"Gifting Books & Music Worldwide"

This book or product is a gift to you from the
author and/or publisher and **The I AM Foundation,**
an educational 501c3 nonprofit.
"Our mission is gifting books and music worldwide."
You can receive great books and products like this
by visiting **www.IAMFoundation.org**.
Please write us at **iam@iamfoundation.org** or
3304 Fourth Ave. San Diego, CA 92103-5704
619.296.2400

Thank you to our sponsor:
The Street Kid Company
www.TheStreetKid.com
"Supporting Kids in Having it all!"

ANN ARBOR MI

Teen Suicide

Look for these and other books in the Lucent
Teen Issues and Overview series:

Teen Alcoholism
Teen Depression
Teen Dropouts
Teen Drug Abuse
Teen Eating Disorders
Teen Parenting
Teen Pregnancy
Teen Prostitution
Teens and Divorce
Teens and Drunk Driving
Teen Sexuality
Teen Smoking
Teen Suicide
Teen Violence

Teen Suicide

by Hayley R. Mitchell

Library of Congress Cataloging-in-Publication Data

Mitchell, Hayley R., 1968–
    Teen suicide / by Hayley R. Mitchell.
        p.   cm. — (Lucent overview series. Teen issues)
    Includes bibliographical references and index.
    Summary: Examines some of the causes of suicidal behavior
in teenagers, including mental health issues and outside pressures,
and discusses prevention efforts and help for survivors.
    ISBN 1-56006-572-9 (lib. bdg. : alk. paper)
    1. Teenagers—Suicidal behavior—United States Juvenile
literature. 2. Teenagers—Suicidal behavior—United States—
Prevention Juvenile literature. 3. Suicide Juvenile literature.
4. Suicide—Prevention Juvenile literature.   [1. Suicide.]
I. Title.   II. Series.
HV6546.M58   2000
362.28'0835—dc21   99-30150
                                                                 CIP

Copyright © 2000 by Lucent Books, Inc.
P.O. Box 289011, San Diego, CA 92198-9011
Printed in the U.S.A.

Contents

Introduction

AT THIS POINT in the history of the United States, at the end of the twentieth century and moving headlong—with computer and electronics technology, medical advancements, and scientific discoveries—into the new millenium, Americans think of themselves as an educated and compassionate society, where citizens can find answers to their questions and help in meeting their individual needs. Why, then, do thousands of American teens take their lives each year? Why do thousands more attempt suicide, feeling there is no help or hope for solving their problems?

Some of the answers to these questions lie in the fact that suicide is still stigmatized in our society. Many people who have lost loved ones to suicide feel shame and a need for secrecy instead of sharing their pain and the lessons of their losses with others. Some people believe the answers also lie in a need for more suicide education. Proponents of such education claim that whether at home, in the schools, or through community efforts, when teens learn about all aspects of teen suicide they are able to see that the problems they face are not theirs alone. When they discover the core causes and symptoms of depression, which often lead to teen suicide, they are moved to seek help for themselves and their loved ones.

By talking about suicide, teens also become aware of the outside forces in their lives that influence their mental health. They can learn to think critically about the music they listen to and the television programs they watch. They can make informed decisions about drinking and about

taking drugs. They can question the need for guns in their homes, guns with which so many teens kill themselves each year.

Some opponents of suicide education fear that talking about teen suicide will only influence more teens to take their lives. Some teens, in fact, have committed suicide after participating in suicide prevention programs at school. While some teens may have been influenced by these so-called contagion factors, many others have been saved by learning that help is available.

Indeed many mental health specialists, parents, teachers, community leaders, and teens themselves have learned that talking about teen suicide today helps prevent suicide in the future. But there are still those who are affected by teen suicide who know little about it, or for whom suicide remains a taboo subject.

Every year thousands of American teens who feel isolated and confused commit suicide. Prevention programs may help to lower this figure.

When people remain silent about suicide, when it remains a source of shame in our society, teens do not have the opportunity to learn, to discuss, to analyze, and to criticize suicide, a topic that affects their friends, their families, and themselves. But when they are offered resources on suicide, as well as support and understanding, they are given both an opportunity and the skills needed to cope with the pressures they face.

1

Teen Suicide Rates Are on the Rise

ACCORDING TO THE Centers for Disease Control and Prevention (CDC), suicide rates among American teens have increased steadily over the past four decades. Although the suicide rate for the general population has remained relatively stable since 1950, the suicide rate for adolescents age fifteen to nineteen jumped 400 percent between 1950 and 1988. Statistics for 1997 suggest that for every suicide in the adult population, there are four suicide attempts. But for every suicide among youths, there are at least one hundred attempts.

While some studies claim that the problem of teen suicide is not as bad as it is often presented, clearly a problem *does* exist. In the United States approximately 40 percent of high school students have contemplated suicide, and 1997 statistics indicate suicide is the third leading cause of death among teens age fifteen to nineteen and the fourth leading cause of death among ten- to fourteen-year-olds. Two thousand teens now commit suicide each year.

What accounts for the increase in teen suicides? The possible causes are as varied as the teens themselves. *Los Angeles Times* urban affairs writer Sonia Nazario says, "Although some suicidal adolescents have obvious mental illnesses, many others show no symptoms of psychological turbulence. They may just be ill-equipped to handle the swiftly shifting realities of growing up in the 1990s."[1]

10

In particular, Nazario notes that many teens no longer view their homes as places of stability. "In many households," she writes, "whether headed by one or two parents, work often is the dominating force, leaving scarce time or energy for deep conversations. Feelings of isolation and rejection often fill the void." Pressures outside the home are also contributors to teen suicide, Nazario says, such as "academic competition, drugs, the push to have sex at younger ages, the obsession to fit in, a drumbeat of songs, movies, and news stories about suicide and violence."[2]

As these issues potentially affect every teen in America, one might wonder why the incidence of suicide among teens is not higher than it already is. Most teens are adequately equipped through their family or community support systems to weather the turbulence of modern adolescence. Other teens, however, are considered at especially high risk for suicide by health care professionals.

Teens who abuse alcohol are at a greater risk for suicide than those who do not participate in such behavior.

These high risk groups include but are not limited to: alcohol and drug abusers; runaways; young African American males; gay or bisexual teen males; and teens who have already attempted suicide on one or more occasions in the past. Gender also appears to be a significant factor in the rate of teen suicide.

Teens who abuse alcohol and drugs are at risk

One group that experts agree are at high risk for suicide are teens who abuse alcohol or other substances. In the general population, 20 to 50 percent of people who attempt or complete suicide abuse drugs, and 15 to 50 percent of people who complete suicide abuse alcohol. These percentages are similarly reflected in the teen population. Statistics gathered in 1997 show that about 42 percent of teen boys and 12 percent of girls who killed themselves had abused alcohol or drugs.

People who abuse drugs and alcohol may do so to escape feelings of depression and loneliness, or to suppress other problems they encounter in their lives. As teens abuse drugs and alcohol, however, their lives ultimately become more complicated. They begin to do poorly or do worse in school; they forgo their responsibilities at part-time jobs or extracurricular activities; and their interpersonal relationships with family and friends suffer. The problems they were trying to escape become worse.

Additionally, many teen abusers do not realize that alcohol (like many drugs) is itself a depressant that can intensify negative feelings. Drugs and alcohol can also cause teens to be more impulsive. By impairing judgment and creating mood swings, drugs and alcohol can blunt the teen's fear of dying, and may turn the contemplation of suicide into a deadly attempt.

Runaways often have nowhere to turn

A second group of teens thought to be at risk for suicide are those who run away from home. Runaways cite a variety of negative experiences in the home that lead them to the streets, including emotional, physical, and sexual abuse; neglect; or other severe problems with family members. When compared with peers who do not run away, these teens are also found to have greater depression and more frequent prior and current thoughts of suicide, and are more likely to be substance abusers.

A 1989 study by researcher A. R. Stiffman found that 30 percent of runaways in the St. Louis area of Missouri reported a past suicide attempt. Likewise, researchers D. Shafer and C. Caton reported in 1984 that 15 percent of the male and 33 percent of the female runaways seeking assistance from a shelter in New York City had made suicide

A nineteen-year-old runaway finds temporary refuge beneath a highway overpass. Such teens lack the stable home life that can help them cope with life's pressures.

attempts. Additionally, 33 percent of teens seeking help had contemplated suicide. These statistics suggest that runaways are at risk, and researcher John M. Davis explains, "it is important to note that these statistics come only from those youth who are served by youth centers. Since these centers see slightly less than 10 percent of the runaway youth population, the problem must be much larger."[3]

Suicide rate of African American males rises

Another group of teens thought to be at risk for teen suicide is African American males. Despite a common misconception in the African American community that suicide is a "white thing," *Jet* magazine reports that in 1996 suicide remained the third leading cause of death among young African American males age fifteen to twenty-four. *Washington Post* staff writer Fern Shen notes that from 1980 to 1993, the suicide rate increased 73 percent for white males age ten to fourteen but it increased 358 percent for black males the same age. For males age fifteen to nineteen, the suicide rate climbed 23 percent for whites and 157 percent for blacks. White males still commit suicide in the highest numbers, but Alex Crosby, an epidemiologist in the Division of Violence Prevention at the CDC, notes that if these trends continue, "suicide rates for young African Americans will be exceeding those of whites within a year or two."[4]

As causes of the increase in suicide among young black males age fifteen to twenty-four, experts most frequently cite drug and alcohol abuse, easy access to guns in many black communities, poverty, unemployment, and racism in the workforce. Preliminary research, however, points in conflicting directions. Shen notes research that suggests that the "surge of suicide springs from social ills [such as poverty] that simply affect black Americans disproportionately" and other studies that suggest that as "American blacks acquire greater social status, they acquire some of the majority white culture's problems [greater numbers of suicides] as well."[5]

Researchers agree that the breakdown of the family structure is often considered a contributor to suicide among black teen males who have not yet entered the workforce or acquired social status. Reverend Cecil L. Murray, pastor of First African Methodist Episcopal Church of Los Angeles, explains that in America, the divorce rate is 50 percent, and the number of out-of-wedlock births nears 75 percent in some poor communities. In this light, "despair is increasing." According to Murray, black teens are often left "without a hands-on mentor . . . [so] the wheel of difficulty keeps spinning more rapidly."[6]

But the absence of a male mentor in the family cannot be the sole cause of suicide among black teens living in disadvantaged communities. Indeed, medical examiner Joye M. Carter, who studies patterns of suicide, suggests that increasing pressures on their mothers may contribute to the teens' contemplation of suicide. Although the suicide rate has not risen among black women, substance abuse among women has increased. "It used to be the mom was the tenacious one who held the family up," Carter says, "and now they're tired, burned out, frustrated . . . and they're leaving the family to fend for itself."[7]

In addition to the absence of role models in the lives of disadvantaged black youths, Crosby of the CDC says that a

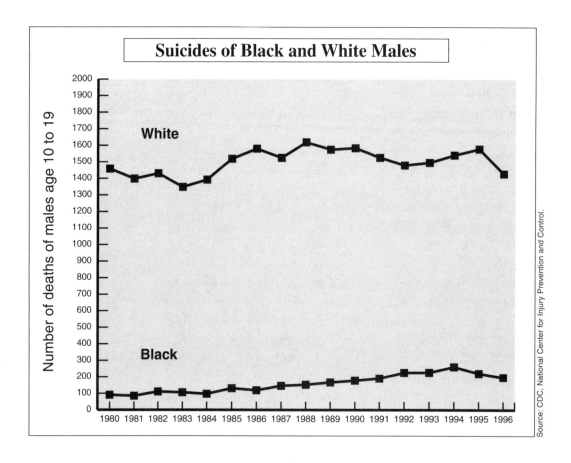

Suicides of Black and White Males

Number of deaths of males age 10 to 19

White

Black

history of violence is another contributing factor to suicide among many black teens. "Children who have been either witnesses or victims of abuse have a greater risk for suicide," he says. "And children who know someone who has completed a suicide are also at risk for suicide."[8]

The African American teens who live in abusive or impoverished environments, or in families with weak infrastructures, often have not acquired the skills to cope with the pain and stress of their everyday lives. Like other teens living in similarly destitute circumstances (suicides among Native American and Latino teens are also steadily climbing), these youths, according to Dr. Frederick B. Philips of the behavioral health firm Progressive Life Center in Washington, D.C., "don't know how to deal with emotional pain. Our youth are lonely, and that is frightening, that is sad. They are depressed. . . . Each day is a struggle to maintain, to hold on, to just get through."[9]

The debate over gay and lesbian teens at risk

Researchers studying suicide often debate whether gay and lesbian teens are more prone to suicidal tendencies than their heterosexual counterparts. In part the issue is contested simply because both suicide and homosexuality are controversial topics; moreover, data on teens who commit suicide may be inaccurate as many gay teens keep their sexual orientation a secret.

Researchers who downplay homosexuality in contributing to teen suicide point to what they view as the scientifically flawed 1989 study by Paul Gibson, published by the Department of Health and Human Services, to make their case. Gibson's study claimed that 30 percent of teen suicides are committed by gay youth, and that three thousand gay teens commit suicide each year. However, his opponents note that since a total of only two thousand teens commit suicide each year, Gibson's figures are inaccurate and exaggerated. Researcher Trudy Hutchens also criticizes Gibson for assuming that all gay teens who commit suicide do so due to what he calls "personal or interpersonal turmoil regarding homosexuality,"[10] when in fact many gay teens who have attempted suicide cite other causal factors for their attempts, such as problems at home.

Researchers who disparage Gibson's work are especially concerned that his findings have been championed by gay activists for political reasons. Using Gibson's statistics, gay rights activists warn that homosexuality must be accepted in our society to prevent further suicides by gay and lesbian youths. While the message of acceptance may be admirable, activists' use of Gibson's unreliable study negatively colors the public's perception of gay teens. "Typically they are portrayed as emotionally vulnerable and as society's victims," Delia M. Rios writes. However, she adds, mental health researchers claim that "most gay and lesbian teens, like teens overall, are emotionally resilient people"[11] who go on to live productive, happy lives.

Researcher Peter Muehrer at the National Institute of Mental Health also worries that "public focus on gay teen suicides might contribute to a phenomenon called 'suicide contagion,' in which troubled gay teens might begin to see suicide as an acceptable way out of their identity struggles."[12]

Gay and bisexual teen males

Despite the controversy surrounding Gibson's study, Dr. Gary Remafedi of the University of Minnesota still believes that gay and lesbian teens should be considered a high risk group for suicide. Although Remafedi's 1997 study concluded that within his study group only 6 percent more lesbian teens had attempted suicide than heterosexual teen girls, it also found that gay and bisexual teen boys ages thirteen to eighteen were seven times more likely to attempt suicide than heterosexual teen males.

Remafedi believes that gay and bisexual teen males attempt suicide in greater numbers because of the negative treatment they receive from society. They may worry about coming out to their parents, or that their parents or friends will learn of and disapprove of their sexual orientation. If their homosexuality is known by others, they may also suffer verbal and physical abuse or outright rejection.

Previous suicide attempters remain at risk

Another group considered to be at high risk for suicide are those teens who have already attempted suicide in the past. If the teen receives no treatment after the first suicide attempt, he or she is considered especially high risk. An indication that teen suicidal behavior should be taken seriously is the fact that one teen in ten who fails to commit suicide ultimately does succeed. Whereas in the adult population, only 1.5 percent of suicide attempters do eventually kill themselves in the future, 15 percent of teen attempters commit suicide in subsequent attempts.

When someone attempts suicide, it can be assumed that he or she already considers suicide a valid option for solving problems. Mental health specialists have extended that logic to include some self-harming behaviors that are not traditionally viewed as suicide attempts but that may indeed indicate a future risk. These behaviors include "accidental" overdose of prescribed medication; a single-car

While researchers continue to debate whether gay and lesbian teens are at high risk for suicide, mental health experts point out that all teens are extremely resilient, regardless of their sexual orientation.

accident, like running into a guardrail or other object at high speed; frequent abuse of alcohol or drugs; or participating in dangerous games, such as street racing or "playing chicken."

Gender differences affect the likelihood of completed suicides

Finally, which teens commit suicide in our society today is also influenced by gender differences among boys and girls. Simply put, of those who attempt suicide, teen boys are more likely to complete the act than teen girls.

A March 1997 study printed in the *Los Angeles Times* reveals that in Los Angeles alone, 36 percent of high school girls, more than one in three, admitted to thinking seriously about committing suicide in the past twelve months. Only 16 percent of boys had thought about suicide. Nationally, these numbers remained similar, with 30 percent of high school girls and 18 percent of boys considering suicide.

Although a significant number of teenage girls may contemplate suicide, statistics show that few of them actually attempt the act.

Fortunately, not all teens who contemplate suicide actually attempt it. This fact may be attributed to school prevention programs, intervention from friends or family, or a teen's ability to work through his or her problems despite thoughts of suicide. Indeed, while 30 percent of high school girls in the nation think seriously about committing suicide, only 12 percent of these girls actually attempt it. Only 6 percent of high school boys attempt suicide, compared to the 18 percent who consider it.

Considering the statistics above, one might assume that more teenage girls kill themselves each year than boys. This assumption, however, is false. The suicide death rate for fifteen- to nineteen-year-olds, per 100,000 teens in the United States, is 18.3 for boys and only 3.5 for girls. The death rate for younger boys committing suicide is more

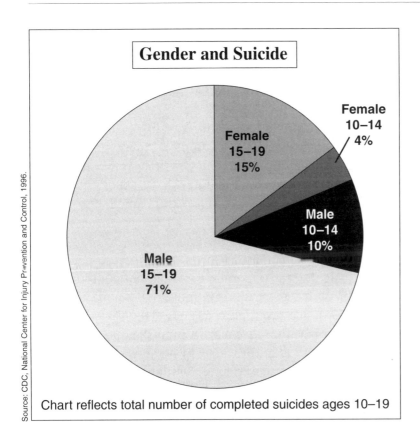

Gender and Suicide

Female 10–14 / 4%

Female 15–19 15%

Male 10–14 10%

Male 15–19 71%

Chart reflects total number of completed suicides ages 10–19

Source: CDC, National Center for Injury Prevention and Control, 1996.

than twice that for younger girls: For boys age ten to four-teen, the suicide death rate is 2.4 per 100,000 teens.

Researchers suggest that the difference in the number of teenage girls and boys attempting and actually completing suicide is related to how these teens are socialized differ-ently in our society. D. K. Curran, author of *Adolescent Suicide Behavior*, says that girls "are encouraged to con-trol angry feelings and withhold aggression." Additionally, they are taught to "rely on others, to accept weakness and dependence on external sources of support."[13] Given this socialization, it is not surprising that girls are more likely to seek help for problems of stress and depression that may lead to suicidal behaviors. Unlike girls, boys in our society are socialized, Curran says, "to express anger and aggres-sion." They are "encouraged to pull themselves up by their bootstraps . . . and to respond to problems with vigor and forthrightness."[14] They are, therefore, much less likely than girls to seek help for their problems.

Researchers claim that these basic differences in gender lead boys to choose more lethal methods of suicide than girls, which accounts for boys' greater rate of suicide completion. For example, boys are more likely to use guns or explosives in their suicide attempts to increase the likelihood of death and prevent the possible humiliation of a failed attempt. Girls are more likely to use poisons, such as sleeping pills, that often prove less deadly.

A warning about labels

Having identified some groups of teens who may be at risk for suicide, it is important to remember not to label all members of these groups—homosexual teens or young black males, for example—as suicidal. Many of these teens do not face the same hardships as their suicidal peers. Statistics help to identify who *may* be at risk and who may benefit from school-based and community suicide prevention programs as well as informal outreach efforts by friends and family members.

On the other hand, it is also essential to note that just because a teen does not fit into any of the listed high risk groups does not mean that he or she will not contemplate or commit suicide. Parents and friends should not assume that their child or friend is immune to suicidal tendencies just because he or she is popular or seems outwardly happy and well adjusted. Neither should parents and friends be unduly alarmed when a teen simply expresses sadness or becomes upset over the normal setbacks of adolescence.

How, then, can suicide risk be distinguished from normal teen worries? The next step in understanding teen suicide is investigating teen mental health and the core issues that lead teens to take their lives.

2

Inner Conflicts

WHILE IT IS helpful to identify populations of teens who are considered at high risk for attempting suicide, it is essential to understand the mental health of all teens. The stresses of adolescence are well recognized: physical and hormonal change coupled with pressures in school and at home, and new, more adult responsibilities such as a part-time job, taking care of siblings, or simply learning to drive.

For some teens, however, the pressures of puberty take a greater toll. Mental health specialist Robert M. Cavanaugh Jr. and his colleagues warn that "while you can count on a teen to be intermittently moody or rebellious, signals such as protracted sadness, persistent high anxiety, or repeated episodes of serious misbehavior merit psychological evaluation."[15]

Depression is a core cause

What seems like average teen worries to outsiders may in fact be depression, one of the core causes of teen suicide. In addition to depression, there are a number of other core causes: Dysfunction in the home, physical abuse, pressure to succeed, interpersonal problems with peers, and financial or legal problems can all create inner conflict for teens. All teens will feel some pressure or anxiety about success, conflicts with peers and parents, and financial responsibilities, and most will not be prone to depression and thoughts of suicide. Those teens who do become suicidal, however, are likely to be highly sensitive to these conflicts. The suicidal teen experiences these difficult situations or stressors as chronic occurrences that ultimately lead to depression.

What causes teen depression and what are the signs of depression? Research shows that 5 to 10 percent of teens in the United States suffer from depression at some time during adolescence, and that half the youths who commit suicide have experienced some form of depression. Without treatment, depression leads to suicide in about 15 percent of depressed teens; yet of the 20 percent of high school teens who are deeply unhappy or who have other psychiatric problems, only one in five will seek professional help. "It is a very difficult time in their lives," says Drew Velting, a psychological sciences professor at Ball State University in Muncie, Indiana. "They are growing

The Symptoms of Clinical Depression

According to the American Psychiatric Association, clinical depression can be diagnosed when someone exhibits five or more of the following symptoms (not related to any medical condition or drugs) during a two-week period:

▶ a depressed mood most of the day, nearly every day

▶ markedly diminished interest or pleasure in most activity during the day, nearly every day

▶ significant weight loss or gain over a month (for instance, a change of more than 5 percent of body weight)

▶ significant change in sleep habits—sleeping far more or far less than usual

▶ extreme agitation or extreme slowness of movement nearly every day

▶ fatigue or loss of energy nearly every day

▶ feelings of worthlessness or excessive guilt every day

▶ diminished ability to concentrate, or indecisiveness nearly every day

▶ recurrent thoughts of death or suicide (or suicide attempts)

up, encountering all sorts of problems. Many think that suicide is the only solution." [16]

Teens who are depressed and teens who are suicidal share many of the same stresses in their lives. One indication that a teen is at risk for a suicide attempt is the expression of negative feelings about him- or herself and a sense of low self-esteem and inadequate accomplishment. Christina, a depressed teen who attempted suicide, says, "I had spells of not caring if I lived or died, and I had to be perfect in school." [17]

External pressures, such as being abused at home, or bullied at school by peers, can also lead to depression in teens. Teens also suffer depression brought on by the divorce of their parents, their own breakup with a girlfriend or boyfriend, or the death of a parent, sibling, or friend. Shelby-Marie, for example, became depressed at age eleven when her mother died. "I ate a lot and thought about death," she says, "and I never seemed to fit in at school." [18] Feeling like they do not fit in is another cause of teen depression. Personal conflicts over sexual orientation, obesity, or other physical differences can heighten feelings of being an outcast.

Four out of five people who kill themselves exhibit signs of depression

Typically, teens indicate serious depression with at least one of a variety of telltale signs. A teen who exhibits any of these signs should be thought of as likely to attempt suicide because four out of five people who kill themselves show these signs of depression before their suicides. First, teens may show an obsession with death. They may think and talk about death a lot more than they did before they became depressed. Making actual suicide threats is another sign of depression that should be taken seriously.

A teen who expresses tremendous feelings of guilt may also be depressed, as might a teen who demonstrates a sudden change in appearance, personality, or behavior. A boy who usually dresses in bright clothes, for example, might take to wearing dark clothing. He may neglect his appearance, and forgo good hygiene or proper grooming. One example of a change in behavior for a depressed teen might be a once active and outgoing girl who suddenly withdraws from family and friends. Instead of participating in her usual activities, she might isolate herself in her room for long periods. A change in her eating and sleeping habits or a dramatic drop in her grades is another sign of depression. Finally, depressed teens who are likely to commit suicide often have a desire to give away their belongings. When someone gives away a prized possession, it is a good indication that that person is contemplating suicide and wants to put his or her life in some kind of order before committing the act.

Teenage depression claims a life

Joey Ortiz was fifteen years old when he hanged himself in the closet of his East Los Angeles home in 1996. Joey was depressed when he killed himself, subject to a variety of pressures and exhibiting more than one of the signs of depression previously discussed.

Joey's mother, Teresa, recalls that although family and friends considered Joey a normal teen, his inner life was in hopeless turmoil, beginning at age seven when his parents separated. As a child, Joey went through a period of bed-wetting after the separation; he had nightmares and was easily brought to tears over minor incidents. Joey grew up to maintain a strained relationship with his father, who had a drinking problem. His father would criticize him if he received less than A's on his report cards, making Joey feel that he would never be good enough in his father's eyes. Joey wrote of these feelings about his father shortly before his death. In poems titled "Death" and "The Call of Death," Joey "wrote that when he looked into his father's eyes, he saw hatred, a wish that Joey were dead. 'I'm always in the shade, never in the light.'"[19]

Depression can trigger suicidal tendencies among people of all ages.

Joey's sixteen-year-old girlfriend Candie offered some solace from the pressures that Joey felt at home, but when she told Joey she was pregnant with his child, new pressures arose and Joey's depression deepened. He told his friend Fabian that he loved Candie and the baby, but he knew he was too young to be a father. He also felt guilty that his mother would be disappointed in him because of the child. "His mother wanted him to excel," Fabian says, "to be better than anybody."[20] Complicating matters, Joey told Fabian that another teen had threatened to kill him over Candie's pregnancy. Everything had just gone wrong.

Under these pressures Joey became increasingly preoccupied with death. In addition to the poems he penned before his death, including one he gave Candie that said he planned to die within a couple of years, Joey spoke aloud of killing himself. He voiced thoughts to Candie about slitting his wrists or dying in a car accident. He even asked her if she had ever considered a suicide pact. Joey asked Fabian what he thought he should do, but clearly he had

Common Warning Signs of Suicide

A suicidal person may:

- talk about committing suicide
- have trouble eating or sleeping
- experience drastic changes in behavior
- give away prized possessions
- have attempted suicide before
- take unnecessary risks
- have had a recent severe loss
- be preoccupied with death and dying
- lose interest in personal appearance
- increase use of alcohol or drugs
- lose interest in hobbies, work, school, etc.
- withdraw from friends and/or social activities
- prepare for death by making out a will and final arrangements

already made up his mind. Shortly before his death he gave away his Nintendo video games to his cousin.

Joey's parents, reunited at the time of his death, remember him storming upstairs on the night of his suicide because he had been forbidden to go out for the evening. Candie recalls that he sobbed to her on the phone. His parents, he said, just didn't understand. In the morning his sister found his body hanging in his closet. Joey exhibited many signs of a depressed teen about to kill himself, but he did not receive intervention for his suicidal thoughts. Had his parents and friends known how to interpret these suicidal messages, Joey's life might have been saved.

Dysfunction at home can lead to mental instability

Author Herbert Hendin writes, "Whether suicidal youngsters retreat to their room or their books or become provocative and defiant, they share a pain, frustration, and anger that most often come from disturbed family relationships."[21] Some of the pressures of home life that can create these disturbed relationships can include abusive parents, alcoholism, financial difficulties, unemployment, and other worries. These pressures can all negatively affect teen mental health, especially when a teen feels unwanted.

Studies suggest that in itself divorce is not a significant factor in the rise in teen suicide, but researchers find that teens who do commit suicide are likely to suffer some form of alienation from their parents. Teens who become suicidal often have grown up in an atmosphere of hostility and resentment. While their families may not be ones that have been broken apart by divorce, according to Hendin, they lack the "reciprocal intimacy, spontaneity, and closeness"[22] that fosters good mental health. In some cases parents may alienate teens because they are unwilling or do not know how to reach out to them. In other cases, teens may alienate themselves from parents through disobedience or self-destructive behaviors such as drug or alcohol abuse.

Difficult teens who are constantly in trouble at school or with the law are sometimes even thought by their families

Dan Foote *Texas International Features*

to be expendable. Parents may grow so tired of their difficulties with such teens that they do not recognize a teen's
risk of suicide. Researcher Joseph Sabbath notes one such
case in which a mother was annoyed by her fifteen-year-
old daughter's constant lying and stealing. "Her mother
frequently told her to drop dead," until one day "she tried
to comply with her mother's wish."[23] This teen's suicide attempt might have been avoided had her family recognized
the girl's disruptive behavior as a need for more positive
attention and recognition at home.

Physical abuse creates inner conflicts

When dysfunction within the family also includes physical or sexual abuse, a teen's mental health suffers even
greater strain. Severe punishment or other physical abuse at
the hands of parents negatively affects teens psychologi-
cally by lowering self-esteem and increasing feelings of

Teens who feel over-whelmed by their stud-ies and the expectations of their parents are likely to exhibit suicidal behavior.

despair and hopelessness. In 1994, researchers estimated that 34 percent of adolescents in outpatient treatment clinics had experienced physical battery by parents or others. And these battered youths are reported to have a 41 percent higher incidence of suicide attempts and other self-destructive behaviors than those who have not been abused.

In addition to battery, sexual abuse is common among adolescents who attempt suicide. In one 1986 study of fourteen girls who had attempted suicide before age thirteen, only one girl had *not* been the victim of some kind of sexual abuse. Like other kinds of physical abuse, sexual abuse severely lowers teens' self-esteem and causes great stress. Suicidal teens who are victims of incest, for example, report a number of conditions that negatively affect their mental states. In addition to feeling self-destructive, these teens may be withdrawn, suffer from hallucinations, feel anxious, and suffer sleep disorders.

Pressure to succeed overwhelms some teens

While some suicidal teens do not get enough attention and support from their parents, others feel smothered by their parents' or society's expectations. For instance, many teens who attempt suicide come from middle- and upper-income families that expect their children to achieve success and status through academics and athletics. These parents are highly driven, says family therapist Susan Davies Bloom. "They are so accustomed to functioning at a high level of control at the office that when they get home, they try to exert the same kind of control."[24]

Children of successful parents often feel their parents have set unrealistic goals for them and give them little room to make mistakes. Andree Brooks, author of *Children of Fast Track Parents*, notes that parents with executive careers strive for perfection. They are often impatient and ruled by efficiency. "Contrast these traits," Brooks says, "with what it takes to meet the needs of a growing child—tolerance, patience, and acceptance of chaos."[25] In an age in which both Mom and Dad might be on the fast track, parents may have so little time for their kids that they hardly know them. Rather than talking about their children's friends and interests when they do spend time together, parents bent on success might ask, "What did you get on your math test?" Teens in this situation can become easily depressed. Committing suicide can become an attractive alternative to living in their parents' shadow.

Even teens who do not come from extremely successful families can feel overburdened by pressures to succeed. Parents, for instance, may unwittingly cause stress by pushing their teens to achieve, to attend better colleges and secure a better future for the entire family. Teens whose friends and siblings are especially accomplished may also suffer low self-esteem by comparison: They feel no matter what they do, they can never measure up. Finally, the pressure to succeed in life

The pressure to succeed in sports and other extracurricular activities can drive some teens to the brink of suicide.

does not always come from outside sources. Sometimes teens who are more driven and greater perfectionists than their peers create this stress for themselves.

Problems with peers

Adolescents normally become less dependent on primary family relationships and more influenced by peers. These relationships can be both stimulating and rewarding as teens gain new interests through their friendships and further develop a sense of themselves. With these new relationships, however, come a new set of anxieties. Adolescents may worry about being popular; they may not know how to deal with pressures to become intimate with girlfriends or boyfriends; or they may encounter pressure to use drugs or alcohol with groups of peers.

Dr. Cynthia R. Pfeffer writes that for teens dealing with interpersonal problems with peers, one of the most crucial precipitators of suicidal thoughts is humiliation. "Feelings of disgrace and public disparagement may shatter a youngster's healthy sense of narcissism [pride] and sense of identity," she says, "and loss of a basic sense of one's worthwhileness is a powerful force to increase thoughts of self-annihilation."[26] At a time when having friends is so crucial to healthy mental development, teens who try but are unable to make friends commonly feel humiliated. In this situation an overweight teen may suffer from being teased by his seemingly popular and athletic male peers. An especially bright student might be labeled the class nerd and excluded from social activities. It is not only the outsiders or loners who suffer from humiliation or other blows to self-esteem; in high school, at a time when fitting in is especially important, opportunities for humiliation abound for everyone.

Some populations of teens who feel they do not fit in with their mainstream peers may seek out groups of friends who are likewise alienated. Teri, a fifteen-year-old whose father died when she was eleven, became increasingly depressed during her adolescence. Her personality changed as she became depressed, and she sought out dif-

Interpersonal problems among peers can cause feelings of isolation and rejection that may lead teens to contemplate suicide.

ferent peers as her old friends increasingly failed to understand her moods.

Teri's mother explains that she became "noncompliant, violated curfews, disobeyed restrictions imposed as punishments, and had run away from home on several occasions." She labeled herself as "stupid," spoke and wrote often of death and suicide, and on three occasions cut her wrists. Her school performance declined and she spoke of hating school. Her peer associations were almost exclusively with other alienated teens, whom she described as "punk and other anarchists."[27]

Financial or legal problems

Another common cause of suicide attempts among teens is the presence of financial or legal problems. Adolescents who are constantly in trouble with the law or school officials, whether for truancy, stealing, drug abuse, or other crimes, may find that they have pushed their family support systems to the limit. The more trouble they cause, the more estranged they become from their families. Teens in

this position do not know how to turn their lives around. Facing mounting legal fines or jail time, they can feel that suicide is the only option to them in a world that has run out of second chances.

Teens do not need to be in legal trouble to face financial difficulties, however. Today's adolescents carry many of the same financial responsibilities as adults. Many have credit cards and car payments, or pay for their own apartments and amenities before they turn eighteen. Sometimes the pressures of these responsibilities can be too much for teens. Credit card debts can mount up quickly, for example, and the money from part-time employment never seems to stretch far enough. Feeling like a failure in the adult world, a teen in financial straits might find it too difficult to turn to parents or friends for support. Such shame and helplessness can lead them to suicide.

A family's financial difficulties can also place undue strain on teens. For one teen in Pennsylvania, receiving a $154 speeding ticket led to suicide. Sixteen-year-old Lambert Hillman received a speeding ticket for driving seventy-four miles per hour in a forty-five-mile zone. His friend's father, Chuck Fowler, stated that Lambert was upset about the ticket because he knew his mother did not have the money to pay the fee. Lambert's stepfather had recently died of cancer, and after the depletion of his medical insurance, the family had been forced to mortgage their home to pay medical costs. "You had a sixteen-year-old kid and he's taking calls from the hospital and the creditors," Fowler said. "He became aware of and involved in things that a kid just shouldn't have to deal with."[28]

In addition to losing his stepfather, injury had hindered Lambert's performance in football and hockey at school. The stress of the parking ticket was too much for the teen after a string of upsets in his life led to depression. Despite Chuck Fowler's offer to pay the speeding fine for him, Lambert jumped from a bridge and drowned himself in the Monongahela River. Unfortunately in this case, those who tried to reach out to Lambert were not aware that he believed himself to be so far beyond help.

Depression, dysfunction in the home, physical abuse, pressure to succeed, interpersonal problems with peers, and financial or legal problems are some of the core causes of teen suicide. Each of these factors affects the mental health of teens by causing alienation, confusion, anxiety, low self-esteem, and negative feelings that lead to states of hopelessness. Inner turmoil is not the only cause of teen suicide, however; a number of outside factors may also influence a teen's decision to end his or her life.

3

Outside Influences

MENTAL HEALTH EXPERTS generally look for psychological causes to explain teen suicide, but other factors that may contribute to teen suicide are not directly related to mental health. Among the more hotly debated factors are the influence of mass media, substance abuse, and the availability of guns. The perceived relationship between these issues and teen suicide has prompted a number of teen advocacy groups to call for tighter government controls in these areas.

Is the media responsible?

In recent decades, suicide researchers have focused on the possible influence of the media on teen suicide. Some teens, these researchers claim, are negatively affected by newscasts, fictional portrayals, or messages about suicide in television, film, and music. This suggestion polarizes the debate into two camps: those arguing for strict government control of the media and those championing free speech issues.

Media watchers accuse television and film producers of inciting teens to commit copycat suicides after viewing extensive, even glamorized coverage of suicides on the news or in movies that contain scenes of suicides. They cite separate studies in 1987, 1992, and 1993 which found an increase in adolescent suicides in the week following highly publicized celebrity suicides in newscasts. The correlation was especially strong when reports of the suicides spanned several days and were aired by a variety of media sources.

(C)Arnold Wiles - Rothco Cartoons   87-16E39

When the suicides of famous people were not given wide media coverage, researchers noted that adolescent suicides did not increase.

Fictional television programs or movies about or containing suicides are reported to increase the rate of teen suicide, but researchers note that findings in this area are not absolute. One 1986 study found that incidence of completed

A scene from the controversial 1978 movie The Deer Hunter. *The movie is believed to have sparked over forty copycat suicides between 1978 and 1986.*

and attempted teen suicide increased in the two weeks after television films about suicide aired in the New York City area. When the study was replicated, researchers noted increases in teen suicide in New York City proper and in Cleveland, but not in Dallas and Los Angeles. In 1988 another study examined the effects of three television films about teen suicide on adolescents in twenty-one cities. The teen suicide rate was the same two weeks before the film aired and two weeks after it was shown. There was, however, an increase in carbon monoxide suicides immediately after one film that depicted this method of suicide.

Two films that have been linked to the phenomenon of suicide contagion are the 1985 made-for-television movie *Surviving* and the Oscar-winning feature *The Deer Hunter*, released in 1978. Starring popular teen actor Molly Ringwald, *Surviving* aired during a period of concentrated media attention on cluster suicides, rashes of suicides by teens in the same school or community in a relatively short period of time. The story depicts two teens who take their lives by carbon monoxide poisoning. Two days after watching the movie, seventeen-year-old David Balogh committed suicide by carbon monoxide poisoning. Friends remember that he was obsessed with the movie and that he had commented about how good it was.

Marcia Wenger's teen daughter Keri also took her life shortly after viewing the film. Wenger is convinced the film influenced Keri's decision to end her life because she left her suicide note in a copy of *People* magazine that featured an article about the film. Wenger remembers that when Keri watched the movie she was "fascinated with the death and with the kids. I think it was almost like her life," she says. "It was giving her the okay." [29]

The Deer Hunter, starring Robert DeNiro and Christopher Walken, contains graphic scenes of Russian roulette—pointing at one's head a gun loaded with a single bullet and pulling the trigger—including one in which Walken's character kills himself. After the television and video release of *The Deer Hunter*, Dr. Thomas Radecki discerned a pattern of accidental or deliberate suicide by people imitating the Russian roulette game featured in the film. Radecki lobbied for broadcasters and video distributors to edit the film, but his warnings went unheeded. The deaths continued. Between 1978 and 1986 Radecki documented forty-three Russian roulette deaths worldwide that imitated the scene in the film which the victims had recently watched. Of these, sixteen were defined as teen suicides and two as accidental deaths of teens.

A possible link

Though data on the influence of visual media on teen suicides is not always conclusive, mental health professionals seem more willing to admit than discount a possible connection. They are quick to note, however, that the effects are not the same for all teens. In the *New England Journal of Medicine*, suicidologists Madelyn Gould and David Shaffer contend, "television broadcasts of fictional stories featuring suicidal behavior *may* [emphasis added] in some cases lead to imitative suicidal behavior among teenagers. . . . The presumptive evidence suggests that fictional presentations of suicide *may* [emphasis added] have a lethal effect." [30]

Because of the possible link and their worries about the effects of television violence in general, a number of children's advocacy groups have worked to secure stricter government control over television broadcast programming. Programmers have retained their rights to free speech, but have reached some compromises by creating television rating systems that mirror those of motion pictures. Many violent or otherwise potentially harmful shows are also now aired at later hours so as not to influence the younger audience.

Singing songs of suicide

In music, just as in film and television, the subject of suicide is addressed frequently. Popular artists including Simon and Garfunkel and Elton John have sung of suicide. Some parents have claimed their children were driven to suicide by suggestive music lyrics or subliminal messages in music, and have sued artists such as Judas Priest and Ozzy Osbourne for damages. The courts in these controversial cases, however, have ruled in favor of the artists, who are protected under the free speech clause of the First Amendment. No causal link has so far been proven between lyrics and teen suicide.

One widely publicized case in the debate over the influence of popular music on teen suicide is the lawsuit brought against British rock group Judas Priest. In December 1985, one Nevada teen, Raymond Belknap, killed himself and another, James Vance, tried to kill himself, after listening to the album *Stained Glass* for six hours.

The parents of the teens brought the suit against Judas Priest, claiming that the song "Beyond the Realms of Death" influenced the boys' suicide pact. Kenneth McKenna, an attorney for the Vance family, states, "The suggestive lyrics combined with the continuous beat and rhythmic, nonchanging intonations of the music combined to induce, encourage, aid, abet, and otherwise mesmerize the plaintiff into believing the answer to life was death."[31]

In addition, the families contended that the song contains the subliminal message "do it," encouraging suicide. This argument was not enough for the court, however. The band's defense was successful in asserting that the suicide pact was,

The suggestive lyrics of Judas Priest's suicide-related song "Beyond the Realms of Death" were the subject of a late-1980s lawsuit.

suicidologist Steven Stack and his colleagues explain, "the ultimate step in a long history of drug abuse, alcohol abuse and the boys' respective highly dysfunctional families."[32]

Not the lyrics but the subculture

Stack suggests that it is not the lyrics of songs that contribute to incidence of suicide, but the subculture of the fans who listen to the music. Stack studied country and heavy metal music subcultures and found a number of elements in those populations that suggested risk for suicide. These elements had the greatest effect on teens in the heavy metal subculture, and it is heavy metal lyrics that have come under the most scrutiny in relation to teen suicide.

Stack notes that the lyrics of heavy metal music often reflect the problems of its fans, primarily white working-class males with problems that already relate to greater than average risk of suicide. The themes underlying much of the music are chaos and pessimism, including emotional trouble such as depression, alienation, and failed personal relationships. "Hopelessness and cynicism pervade the songs of metal and the fans are often attracted to it since it reinforces their own alienation," Stack writes. "Hopelessness is a principal psychological state conducive to suicide, considerably more important than depression."[33]

Heavy metal fans seem to relate to these feelings of helplessness. Researchers also find that heavy metal fans are more inclined to support life-risking or reckless behavior. In one study, 62 percent of these fans said they supported children under age ten listening to songs about suicide, murder, or satanism. In the general population of rock fans, only 32 percent of those polled found these topics suitable for kids. Finally, family dysfunction was also found to be more prevalent among heavy metal fans, and it may contribute to their attraction to the music. Fans of heavy metal report more problems with parents and are more likely to come from broken homes or single mother homes than are fans of other music.

In light of these findings, mental health professionals hold that it is not that the lyrics of songs themselves cause suicidal behavior among the subcultures of fans, but that "they fall on the ears of an adolescent who is already—because of home, family, and school problems, delinquency, substance abuse, etc.—a moderate or even high risk for suicide."[34]

On the other hand, some studies describe teens who claim that listening to heavy metal music actually helped prevent them from committing suicide. They say the music purged them of aggression or feelings of depression. The majority of studies in this area, however, concur that the subculture is characterized by high risk for suicide. These findings prompted the Parents' Music Resources Center, a group led in part by Tipper and then-senator, now vice president Al Gore in 1985, to present their case in special Senate hearings. Arguing that heavy metal music promoted suicide and other social problems among adolescent listeners, the group called for placing warning labels about explicit lyrics on heavy metal album covers. Other groups have gone as far as sponsoring mass burning of such albums, and finally, the Federal Trade Commission has issued warnings about heavy metal music to broadcasters.

Suicide and substance abuse

As noted in Chapter 1, teens who abuse drugs or alcohol are considered high risk for suicide attempts. Adolescents who are depressed may turn to alcohol or drugs to reduce their feelings of hopelessness, but may not realize that using these may reduce the inhibitions that might otherwise prevent them from committing suicide. In this light, alcohol and drugs make it easier for teens to express their anxieties through suicidal behavior. Although teens may turn to alcohol and drugs to relieve some inner turmoil, these substances work as negative outside forces and affect their ability to make decisions.

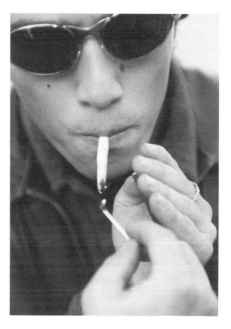

Health specialists note that teen use of alcohol and drugs often leads to hostile and aggressive behavior, and is a way of demanding immediate attention in a world that appears indifferent to individual distress. These behaviors are signs of teens who are unable to deal with the stresses in their lives and can be considered a slow form of suicide. Philip Patros and Tonia Shamoo write of one angry teen named Scott who alienated himself in this way:

Rather than serving as an escape, drug use compounds a teen's feelings of isolation and hopelessness while also clouding his or her decision-making abilities.

> He disrupted classes, rebelled against family and school, and was in trouble with the law for the use of drugs and alcohol. Instead of this behavior satisfying his anger and frustrations, it made him all the more isolated since many of his peers wanted nothing to do with him. Not seeing his behavior as responsible for the alienation he suffered, he blamed others and became more involved with drugs and alcohol. Feeling unable to adjust to his environment, he felt the only solution was suicide.[35]

Like many teens, Scott turned to drugs and alcohol to ease his frustrations, but the more involved he became with these substances, the greater grew his problems. Mental health specialists would say his actions were a call for help, but Scott had alienated himself so much by his increasingly self-destructive behavior that those around him were less and less apt to listen.

Many studies on suicide in adolescents find that not only are many suicidal teens involved in alcohol and drugs in general, many use these substances at the time of their suicide attempts. One study in 1982, for example, found that adolescents are ten times more likely than younger children or adults to use alcohol or drugs immediately preceding their suicidal behavior. This fact supports the idea that the use of alcohol and drugs helps motivate teens to end their lives.

Firearms are the predominant method of suicide

While some teens turn to drugs as a method of committing suicide by overdose, the predominant instrument of suicide for both boys and girls in the United States is the firearm. According to 1997 national statistics, 58 percent of suicide attempters age ten to fourteen chose firearms and other explosives as their method of suicide, as did 71 percent of those age fifteen to nineteen.

A teen's method of suicide directly correlates with his or her willingness to die. The more a teen is intent on dying, the more lethal is his or her choice of the method of suicide. Death is more certain by hanging or gunshot, for example, than by overdose ingestion, carbon monoxide poisoning, or wrist slashing. The fact that so many of our nation's teens are choosing the most lethal of methods suggests they are serious in their intentions to die. Other factors that might influence a teen to choose a firearm as a method of suicide are the accessibility of guns and the teen's knowledge of, experience, and familiarity with their use.

Many call for gun control to prevent teen suicide

Although to say the presence of guns in our society is a cause of teen suicide is controversial, firearm accessibility does appear to contribute to the high success rate of teen suicides. In light of this, many advocates of adolescent suicide prevention programs are in favor of strict gun control measures across the nation.

Gun control groups focus on statistics such as these to make their case: In the United States, half of the homes contain at least one firearm. And every year, 1,400 youths age ten to nineteen are killed with these weapons accidentally or as a means of suicide. In 1990, for example, the National Center for Health Services recorded 2,237 suicides among ten- to nineteen-year-olds. Of these, 142 youths age ten to fourteen and 1,332 teens age fifteen to nineteen used guns to kill themselves. Among those who attempt suicide, adolescents are known to be the most impulsive: If they have the desire to commit suicide and a quick method is available, they will choose it without lengthy consideration. Those who argue for gun control as a form of suicide prevention believe that if guns were not available at home, teens attempting suicide could not act on their impulses as easily, and would have to use less sure, more fallible methods which might ultimately save their lives.

Others feel gun control will not prevent teen suicide

Despite a number of studies that suggest the risk of suicide increases when there is access to guns in the home, some gun control opponents believe that tighter government

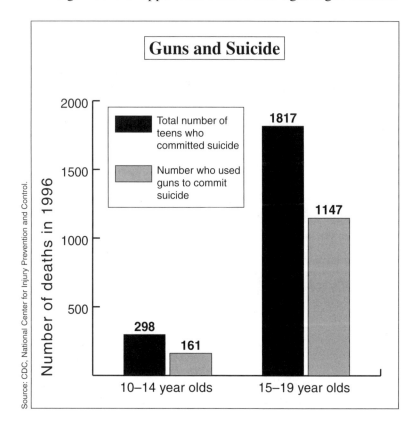

Source: CDC, National Center for Injury Prevention and Control.

Demonstrators protest against gun-related violence. In America, the majority of teens who commit suicide do so with the aid of a gun.

controls of guns will do little to decrease the teen suicide rate. After studying suicide rates and gun control laws in U.S. cities with populations of over 100,000 people, criminologist Gary Kleck reported in 1991 that although gun control laws did affect the rate of suicide by guns, the total rate of suicide remained the same.

This finding correlates with the belief of many gun control opponents that if someone wants to commit suicide, he or she is going to do so no matter what. If guns are not accessible, those who attempt suicide will choose another method. To support this argument, opponents of gun control point to the examples of other countries. In Japan, for instance, firearms are tightly controlled by the government and are extremely difficult to acquire. That nation, however, has a 30 percent higher incidence of teen suicide than the United States. Teens in Japan are finding other ways to kill themselves; gun control has not prevented these suicides. As the debate rages about whether gun control can prevent teen suicide, one thing remains clear: American teens who commit suicide are more and more frequently turning to guns.

Along with alcohol, drugs, and the media, guns remain a potential external force that has the power to influence some teens who take their lives. Each of these outside influences mainly affects individual teens. Other factors, however, are known to influence groups of teens who fall into other categories of suicide phenomena.

4

Suicide Phenomena

TEENS WHO COMMIT suicide may be influenced by their own depression, dysfunction in the home, interpersonal problems, the media, drug or alcohol abuse, and other factors that affect them as individuals. Sometimes, they are also influenced by other teens. The phenomena of suicide pacts and cluster suicides should not be overlooked in the discussion of teen suicide. Although elements of the two phenomena often overlap, defining the two separately is helpful. Suicide pacts are promises made between friends who agree to commit suicide together. Suicide clusters are rashes of suicides by teens in the same school or community in a relatively short period of time.

Making a promise to die

Sometimes suicidal teens discover peers who have similar feelings of helplessness. Rather than finding solace in knowing there are others who share these feelings, however, some teens make and deliberately carry out pacts with each other to end their lives.

One much-studied suicide pact occurred in Bergenfield, New Jersey, in 1987. In this case, seventeen-year-old Cheryl Burress, her sixteen-year-old sister Lisa, and their friends Thomas Olton, age eighteen, and Thomas Rizzo, age nineteen, committed suicide. They died by carbon monoxide poisoning in a vacant housing project garage frequented by teenagers as a place to drink alcohol and smoke marijuana.

Shortly before the teens' suicide, their friend Joseph Major had fallen from a cliff to his death. Some authorities suspected that his death was a suicide, but it was ruled an alcohol-related accident by police. After the suicide of the four teens, family and friends questioned whether their pact grew out of Joseph's death. Lisa, for instance, had dated the boy and often visited his gravesite. While grief can have a powerful effect on teens, experts doubt that grief alone influenced the teens' suicide. In fact, all of the teens exhibited risk factors for suicide before their deaths, including previous suicide attempts, drug and alcohol abuse, depression, and problems at home and at school. Three of the teens had already dropped out of the local high school, and one of them had just been suspended. Their deaths, however, remained a shock to the community.

They seemed like normal girls

Sometimes the risk factors for suicide are not as apparent as in the Bergenfield case, but they are often not far beneath the surface. More recently, in February 1995, two teens in Victorville, California, Jennifer Powell and Annette Sander, also took their lives in an apparent suicide pact. They coined their pact "Project Mushroom," and wrote about it in numerous letters that family members

One of the Bergenfield suicide victims is wheeled from the car in which the teens carried out their grisly suicide pact.

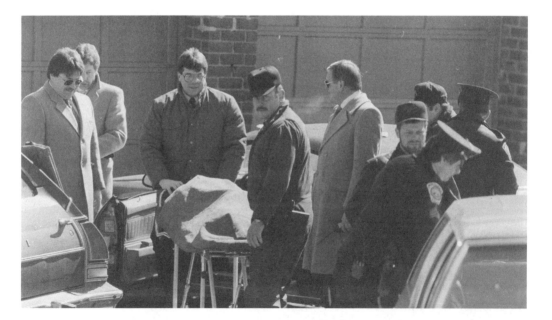

discovered after their deaths. These notes, *People Weekly* reporter Ron Arias writes, are "astonishingly banal, mixing talk of death with breezy comments about homework, boyfriends, and hair." [36]

By outward appearances, Jennifer and Annette were average middle-class teens with an average share of normal teen worries. They were both honor-roll students, excelled at sports, and were active in other extracurricular activities. In their letters, however, both girls admitted that they were sick of life. The girls did not specifically note what was painful in their lives, but they did make the point that their suicide was not a stunt to get attention. They wanted out, and they had decided to go together.

"It's like no one cares about me"

While friends and family were shocked by the suicides, there were some early signs that at least one of the girls was in trouble. A few months before her suicide, Jennifer drastically changed her attitude and appearance. She stopped seeing her old friends and started to hang around a group of punk and grunge rock fans at school. She dyed her brown hair black, blue, and blonde, started wearing a lot of black, and talked often about witchcraft. In her letters to Annette, she wrote frequently of death and suicide. Though occult activities are not suspected as influences in the suicides, Annette also had a preoccupation with witchcraft. Like Jennifer, Annette also discontinued many of her friendships before her suicide.

Friends and family may have been unaware of it at the time, but the girls suffered from inner turmoil that they discussed in letters written before carrying out their suicide pact. Jennifer, who wrote that she had confessed to her mother that she had attempted suicide in the past, clearly felt that she was expendable in her family. "I bet when Project Mushroom goes off, nobody would ever care," she wrote of her impending suicide. "They won't even know I'm gone. It's like no one cares about me." [37] Annette noted that she felt ugly despite the fact that she had had boyfriends in the past who found her attractive. "I always wanted to kill myself," she wrote, and when she met Jennifer she found companionship in "someone who feels the same as I do."[38]

Suicide pacts and clusters: the contagion theory

Some researchers who studied suicide pacts and clusters in the 1980s, feel that a contagion factor plays a role in suicide pacts and cluster suicides. "Kids who are depressed and sitting on the fence," says psychologist David Clark, "don't need much of a nudge. The suicide death of one young person makes it easier for the next one."[39] Annette, for instance, found it easier to kill herself after she met Jennifer, who often talked of suicide. In cluster suicides, teens affected by contagion are influenced directly when actually knowing the victim of a preceding suicide, or indirectly by hearing about the suicide of others through news reports or word of mouth.

Physician Lucy Davidson at the CDC (Centers for Disease Control and Prevention) agrees with Clark and worries about the role of the media in spreading this contagion. Kids who are suicidal to begin with may see the attention a suicide story receives in the media and seek out similar notoriety. "They begin to think that maybe if they [do] it, it will have an impact and will be noticed," Davidson says. "People think rationally most of the time, but [are] not so rational when thinking about suicide. They think they'll be around to watch the community react, and they don't really appreciate that they'll be dead."[40]

Suicide clusters in the news

One of the reasons the Bergenfield case still receives attention is that after the teens' deaths, other suicides occurred that were thought to be related to the case. Two days after the Bergenfield deaths received media attention, two other teens killed themselves in a similar manner in a small suburb of Chicago. Within a week of the teens' suicide, a fourteen-year-old boy from another Chicago suburb also died in his car, and news clippings of the Bergenfield case were found in his room. Also within the same week, similar suicides were reported in Illinois, Nebraska, and Washington. A suicide contagion seemed to have taken hold.

Likewise, after Jennifer and Annette killed themselves in Victorville, teens from the same town tried to follow suit. Seventeen-year-old Julie Banks, who had been treated for manic depression, succeeded in taking her life. And sixteen other teens attempted suicide within seven months of Jennifer and Annette's suicide pact. Most of these girls were ninth graders who admitted to feeling depressed and rejected by friends. School administrator Ron Powell notes that the contagion effect should not be discounted in these cases. "After a suicide, other kids see it as an option," he says. "They see the attention it gets and think, 'Wow, this is how I could end my pain—I could go out with a bang.'"[41]

A community of suicides: Pierre, South Dakota

One U.S. town that has felt the devastation of suicide contagion is Pierre (pronounced "peer"), South Dakota. Since 1995, eight teens and three others under age twenty-three have killed themselves in Pierre. In a city of only thirteen thousand people, this suicide rate is about thirteen times greater than the national average.

Pierre is a safe town. It has seen one murder in nine years, and residents there are used to leaving their doors unlocked. Residents are shocked that so many teens have killed themselves, and mental health experts cannot explain these apparent cases of suicide contagion. Dr. Madelyn Gould, who was drawn to the case, questions, "Why do you have a suicide in one community and nothing else happens, and why do you have another community where one suicide follows another? We haven't found any striking pattern. We've seen it in affluent areas and poor areas, in rural communities and urban communities."[42]

Distraught friends of Cheryl and Lisa Burress, victims in the highly publicized Bergenfield suicide pact, console each other outside of the sisters' funeral home.

The suicides in Pierre are especially difficult to understand because suicide risk factors were not apparent in many of the teens who killed themselves, and the suicides, committed a few months apart from each other, seem unrelated except for their occurring in the same town. Of the eight teens, only one had been in therapy for depression, two had possible problems with alcohol, and one suffered a learning disability that affected his self-esteem. After they had heard of other deaths in Pierre, however, at least two of the teens who later committed suicide had mentioned to their families that they would never consider it.

Teens in Pierre had nowhere to turn

One recent death in Pierre that was especially shocking to the community is that of fifteen-year-old Kenny White, who committed suicide on December 2, 1997. Kenny's mother states that he seemed to be enjoying his teen years; his friends note that he always seemed happy, although, like most teens who commit suicide, Kenny felt under pressure. From the outside, the stresses in his life might seem unlikely to cause him to commit suicide, but the weight of his problems collectively were too much for him.

Reporter Margaret Nelson explains Kenny's emotional turmoil: "He'd broken up with his girlfriend a week earlier, and the day before he shot himself, he'd gone to the funeral of a friend killed in a car accident. He was also juggling schoolwork and two part-time jobs to make truck and insurance payments."[43] High school student Nicole Cholik expresses an understanding of Kenny's pressures. She adds, "Riggs is a tough high school. You're expected to accomplish great things. There was a taboo on seeking help for emotional things."[44]

One theory about the cause of Pierre's rash of suicides is that the town offers little in the way of mental health services to its residents. There is no practicing psychiatrist in the town, for example, and the nearest medical center that offers mental health services to teens is over two hundred miles away. Teens were unable to receive immediate care for their emotional problems. The suicides have prompted

DON'T RIDE WITH STRANGERS...

some changes in the community, but as recently as 1998, suicidal people who called 911 for assistance were put in jail because there were no other facilities in town to keep them until they could be evaluated by health care professionals. Those who have lost loved ones to suicide in Pierre also have no local support systems. After one teen committed suicide, her family had to wait eighteen months for a spot to open up for them in a suicide support group in another town.

Today, however, the future is beginning to look a little brighter for the residents of Pierre. Students, parents, and city officials have created a suicide prevention committee that meets in the Chamber of Commerce, and the city has been linked to a suicide hotline in Sioux Falls. Other preventative measures include suicide intervention classes for all residents, mentor programs, and public service announcements. Active students have also sponsored visiting speakers who address self-esteem issues.

Some guidelines for media reporting of suicides

Increasing mental health services may be especially helpful for towns that have suffered high teen suicide rates. Suicide contagion may also be curtailed with the help of the media. Columbia University's David Shaffer, professor of psychiatry and pediatrics, has studied suicide clusters. In his studies he found that many who attempted suicide had had recent personal contact with a friend or other adolescent who was suicidal. In the 1980s Shaffer urged communities to withhold news of suicides from the media and to refrain from large community meetings or school assemblies that would draw more attention to a local teen suicide.

Today, in a world in which media coverage is omnipresent, Shaffer's recommendation may seem a bit unrealistic. However, in a 1994 national workshop on suicide contagion and the reporting of suicide in the media, members of the CDC concurred that, when reporting a suicide the media can follow certain steps to reduce the likelihood of contagion.

First and foremost, media and health professionals should work together to ensure responsible and accurate reporting. They should refrain from repetitive coverage of a suicide which may promote preoccupation of suicide among at-risk teens, and reports should not try to offer simplistic explanations of suicide. Claiming that a youth committed suicide because of a breakup with a boyfriend or girlfriend, for example, is not sufficient, as people who commit suicide most often have a history of other problems that lead up to the suicidal behavior.

Cluster suicides might also be prevented if the media would refrain from sensational coverage or reports that glorify suicide victims. Limiting morbid details, photographs, and technical details about the method of suicide is one way to cut down on sensationalizing. Likewise, human interest stories that focus on a community's expression of grief after a suicide might have negative consequences. "Such actions," the CDC reports, "may contribute to suicide contagion by suggesting to susceptible persons that society is honoring the suicidal behavior of the deceased person, rather than mourning the person's death."[45]

Similarly, reports that strive for empathy with the suicide's family and friends should avoid descriptions of the positive aspects of a victim's life or character. The CDC notes, "If the suicide completer's problems are not acknowledged in the presence of these laudatory statements, suicidal behavior may appear attractive to another at-risk person—especially those who rarely receive positive reinforcement for desirable behaviors."[46]

Media coverage can help others

While recommending these actions for the reporting of suicides in an effort to prevent cluster or copycat suicides,

Police officers assemble outside of Columbine High School in Littleton, Colorado, after two teens opened fire on students and faculty and then committed suicide on April 20, 1999.

A mother and son grieve at the makeshift memorial erected at Littleton's Columbine High School. Media hype over other school shootings may have prompted the Columbine tragedy.

the CDC acknowledges that media reports of suicides can benefit communities if the reports are handled responsibly. "An ongoing dialogue between news media professionals and health care and other public officials is the key to facilitating the reporting of this information,"[47] the CDC claims. One positive benefit of news reporting is the potential to highlight community efforts to address the problem of suicide.

News coverage, for instance, might describe community support groups that are available for suicidal teens or grieving families, or they might offer information about suicide risk factors. These less sensational approaches to covering suicides in the media are just a few of a number of the positive steps that our society can take to help prevent teen suicide.

5

Prevention Programs and Treatment

MANY PEOPLE VIEW suicide a topic that should not be discussed. Some who have lost friends and family to suicide may feel sufficiently disgraced that they try to hide the fact of the suicide from others. In order for suicide prevention and treatment programs for teens who have already attempted suicide to work, however, people must be willing to talk about suicide.

Psychiatrist Lloyd B. Potter and his colleagues note,

> By communicating with parents, teachers, and youth about recognizing suicide risk and appropriate action to take when risk is perceived, we may begin to see positive effects in the reduction of youth suicide. In addition, by communication with the public about the magnitude of the problem and the preventability of suicide, support for developing a strong scientific base for prevention may grow.[48]

Once our society is able to talk more openly about suicide, more suicidal teens may come forward with their feelings of hopelessness, and we will be better able to get them appropriate help.

Much can be done in the areas of suicide prevention and treatment to increase teens' chances of finding this help. First, parental intervention is especially important in prevention efforts. Some communities, however, realize that parental intervention is not always available to teens. Therefore, residents in a variety of cities and towns throughout the nation have begun their own grassroots programs for suicide prevention. As we will see, large corporations like the Ronald McDonald House Charities are also doing their share.

Many communities are also emphasizing the role of teachers in preventing teen suicide. Although some groups are adamantly opposed to the process, more and more teachers are receiving suicide prevention training, and more of these teachers are discussing suicide prevention in their classrooms as part of their standard curriculum. School-based health clinics have also been effective in suicide prevention. In these clinics, students can talk confidentially to trained mental health specialists about their problems. Finally, traditional suicide hotlines also continue to help in prevention efforts.

All of these prevention efforts are also effective in the treatment of teens who have already attempted suicide. In many cases, however, further intervention is required to ensure the safety of the at-risk teen. For instance, hospitalization may be necessary to stabilize a teen's mental health. Individual and family therapy is another important component in treating suicidal teens.

A parent's watchful eye

Open lines of communication with parents is vital for suicidal teens, but teens do not always feel that their parents understand their needs. One father lost his seventeen-year-old son after his third suicide attempt. In hindsight he wishes that he could have made himself more clearly available to him. "My son was terrified of taking sole responsibility for his future, and somehow I failed to convey that I would support his future efforts. People in pain need to know they're being heard."[49]

Mental health specialists emphasize the need for parents to understand that their teens do not yet have the tools and skills to handle their problems. In addition, what may seem like small problems to parents may sometimes seem insurmountable to teens. Teens cannot always see that these problems are temporary ones, that some issues have a way of working themselves out. Parents are encouraged

With support and communication, parents can help their teens overcome stresses and suicidal feelings.

to help teens discover solutions to what seem like the smallest of problems.

The key for parents to help their teens is to learn to recognize the signs of depression and suicidal behavior. Depression, alcohol or drug abuse, anxiety, and other disorders that can lead to suicidal thinking can all be treated.

All suicide prevention programs warn parents and others involved in the lives of teens to take all direct suicide threats seriously. Parents and friends of teens should also be aware of more indirect threats, such as a teen expressing the feeling that the family would be better off without him. In these cases, parents are urged to intervene, to make sure teens know their support is there for them and that they will work to find them the help they need. The majority of people who get help for their suicidal feelings do recover when the causes of those feelings are discovered and treated appropriately.

Community grassroots efforts

Some of this help can be found in community grassroots efforts. In September 1994, Dale and Darlene Emme returned home to discover the suicide of their teenage son. Since then, they have devoted their lives to suicide prevention efforts in their hometown of Westminster, Colorado. Part of their efforts included the creation of the Yellow Ribbon Program, which has worked to distribute over 100,000 cards that contain suicide prevention information for youths.

One side of the card states that the bearer is considering suicide. It serves as a voice for teens who are in trouble but may be too overwhelmed to talk about their problems. Teens simply present the card to someone they feel can help them. The back of the card informs adults or peers what the cards and program are so they can respond appropriately and immediately if they receive a card from a teen. The Yellow Ribbon cards can also be customized to include local crisis information. This allows youths to receive help in their own home area.

The Yellow Ribbon Program represents the effort of just one of many groups throughout the nation involved in grassroots suicide prevention. People like the Emmes have been instrumental in setting up support groups for suicidal persons or the families of suicide victims and in publicizing the problem of teen suicide through local candlelight vigils and appeals to Congress to recognize and declare suicide, and teen suicide especially, a national problem.

Jerry Weyrauch formed the Suicide Prevention Advocacy Network (SPAN) in Marietta, Georgia, after the suicide of his daughter in 1987. Impressed by the efforts of Mothers Against Drunk Driving in spreading its message against drinking and driving, the Weyrauchs strive for similar success in suicide prevention. SPAN organizes suicide prevention awareness days in numerous communities, and in 1996 the organization delivered over six thousand letters to Congress that urged the government to develop a national suicide prevention program.

In 1997 SPAN planned to deliver thirty-two thousand letters to Congress, each representing an American life lost to suicide each year, in an effort to win government support of suicide prevention efforts. Currently Washington is the only state in the nation that maintains a budget for an official statewide suicide prevention program. The Washington State Youth Suicide Prevention Committee grew out of the grassroots efforts of Scott and Leah Simpson, whose son committed suicide in 1992.

Washington's program recommends broadening school-based suicide prevention programs and reducing teen access to guns and other lethal means of suicide. In addition to these goals, the program has at the root of its educational campaign a very simple message: "Ask the question." Lives have been lost simply because no one thought to ask a teen if he or she was considering suicide. Asking the question can be the first step to intervention.

Gail E. Brandt, who coordinates the suicide prevention program for Washington's Department of Health, says,

U.S. surgeon general David Satcher discusses the nation's efforts to curb suicide during a 1998 press conference held by the Suicide Prevention Advocacy Network.

"Be direct about using the word suicide. Say, 'I'm concerned about you . . . are you thinking about suicide?'"[50] The American Association of Suicidology agrees with this approach. The association's literature adds that teens considering suicide should not be condemned for their feelings; they should be asked to explain the reasons for their feelings instead.

Teens at risk should also be asked if they have considered a method of suicide and if they have made specific plans to carry out their suicide attempt. If a teen answers yes to any of these questions, he or she should be taken to a suicide prevention center, or any available crisis center im-

What to Do

Here are some ways to be helpful to someone who is threatening suicide:

▶ Be direct. Talk openly and matter-of-factly about suicide.

▶ Be willing to listen. Allow expressions of feelings. Accept the feelings.

▶ Be nonjudgmental. Don't debate whether suicide is right or wrong, or feelings are good or bad. Don't lecture on the value of life.

▶ Get involved. Become available. Show interest and support.

▶ Don't dare him or her to do it.

▶ Don't act shocked. This will put distance between you.

▶ Don't be sworn to secrecy. Seek support.

▶ Offer hope that alternatives are available but do not offer glib reassurance.

▶ Take action. Remove means, such as guns or stockpiled pills.

▶ Get help from persons or agencies specializing in crisis intervention and suicide prevention.

Source: American Association of Suicidology.

mediately. Friends and family should not feel disloyal for forcing intervention on a reluctant teen; that intervention can save a life.

A corporate giant lends a big hand

In addition to grassroots prevention programs like SPAN and the Washington State program, some U.S. corporations also acknowledge the need for more suicide intervention for the nation's youth. Ronald McDonald House Charities began funding youth suicide prevention programs and research in 1994, including a $3.2 million study at the University of Illinois. In 1997 Ronald McDonald House also distributed more than thirty thousand suicide prevention CD-ROMs to middle and high schools throughout the nation. In addition, the corporation sponsors a program in Chicago that guarantees support for teens already identified as at risk for suicide. The program provides each teen with a counselor and a team of members who follow up on the teen's progress and his or her family's involvement in recovery for six months. Researchers and educators are indebted to grants such as this because they know the difficulty of raising money for suicide prevention. Many large corporations are wary of having their names associated with suicide in any form because the topic is still considered largely taboo.

Prevention in the schools

Suicide prevention in the schools is a controversial topic because many parents and administrators fear that talking about suicide at school will create suicidal behavior in students who might not otherwise have considered committing suicide. Some parents have even sued school districts, blaming suicide prevention efforts for the deaths of their children.

California schools are the most active in classroom suicide prevention efforts. As of 1997, 41 percent of the state's school districts had suicide prevention programs in place, while the national average is estimated at 15 percent. These efforts stem from the fact that Los Angeles alone has a suicide attempt rate above the national average.

Classroom discussions of suicide and its prevention remain controversial topics in America's schools.

In 1994 the national average for completed suicides among teens fifteen to nineteen was 11.1 suicides per 100,000 people; in California it was 7.5 suicides per 100,000. But the suicide rate for teens in Los Angeles County alone exceeded those of the state at 7.99 suicides per 100,000. In 1996 the Los Angeles school district identified two thousand at-risk students among its ranks.

Katie Owens teaches suicide prevention to her eighth graders at Magruder Middle School in Torrance, Los Angeles County. She asks her class what might cause teens to commit suicide, and they are quick to answer with a variety of responses. Some of these kids already know others who have committed suicide. As in similar classes around the state, Owens presents suicide statistics to her students and teaches them how to recognize friends who might be at risk. Students are urged to tell adults if they or their friends have suicidal tendencies.

Some claim suicide prevention leads to more suicides

Although teachers are trained in suicide prevention before teaching it in their schools, some parents and administrators believe that the mental health of teens should not be the business of teachers. While some people feel the teachers simply are not qualified for the job of suicide prevention, others note that sometimes they go too far in their approach.

Indeed, many who oppose these programs agree with Phyllis Schlafly, the president of the Eagle Forum, a conservative group lobbying against suicide prevention programs in schools. Schlafly feels that rather than teaching suicide prevention to all teens, at-risk teens should be singled out for help. "If one kid has a headache," she says, "you don't give the whole class an aspirin."[51] Ultimately, she feels that suicide prevention should be handled at home.

Schlafly's group and others like it take issue with some teachers' more creative approaches to teaching suicide prevention. In order to teach the finality of death, for example, some teachers have their students write their own suicide notes or obituaries. Some classes have even taken field trips to the morgue. But not only parents and conservative groups oppose these methods; some students find that teachers go too far as well. In Calistoga, Florida, one fifth-grade student returned home in tears after her teacher asked everyone to draw their own headstones with their dates of death. When she refused, the teacher said she would not be excused for lunch until she finished. The student complied by predicting her death in two thousand years.

Phyllis Schlafly (center), president of the conservative Eagle Forum, lobbies against school suicide prevention programs, advocating that such issues should be broached by parents, not teachers.

Ultimately, the most serious concern about these suicide prevention methods is that they can lead to more suicides. Many classes in suicide prevention have shown films such as *Nobody's Useless*, in which a disabled boy is teased at school and then tries to commit suicide by hanging after he overhears his father calling him useless. Deborah Nalepa's eight-year-old son Stephen hanged himself in his room the day after viewing the film. Nalepa claims her son was not depressed. "You put something like this in front of children," she says, "and they are going to re-create it."[52]

Dr. David Shaffer agrees that classroom suicide prevention programs are not the way to go. He approves instead recognizing at-risk teens and working to give them individual support. In particular, he objects to the presentation of suicide: "Prevention courses erroneously present suicide attempts as a fairly common reaction to intense stresses, not as a deviant act by the mentally ill. The effect of this is that a child may come to believe that suicide is normal, even acceptable."[53]

School-based health clinics

Despite the opposition to classroom-centered suicide prevention programs, advocates note that they have made a difference. Between 1970 and 1994 suicides for teens age fifteen to nineteen dropped 39 percent in the city of Los Angeles while the national rate for that age group doubled. Another approach that seems to be making a difference is the creation of school-based mental health clinics for teens. Students can drop in to these clinics without parental authorization. Here, they might discuss ways to boost their self-esteem or cope with stress and anger.

Such centers, like the one housed in a small trailer on the campus of Woodrow Wilson High School in Long Beach, California, are slowly springing up on school campuses across the country. Most offer an array of services such as group and individual counseling for suicide and violence prevention. Some students are referred to these centers by their teachers, school nurses, or counselors who may recognize that teens seem to have an emotional problem the center might help with; others such as teens who need help with anger management skills are sent as a disciplinary measure. As in any therapeutic setting, the teens' problems are kept strictly confidential.

Calls in the night

Suicide hotlines, usually housed in crisis centers, offer immediate assistance to teen callers on the verge of taking their lives. Many centers are open twenty-four hours a day. Teen counselors in teen-operated hotlines are trained in suicide prevention and supervised by mental health specialists or other trained adults.

Teens who call the hotlines often feel more comfortable talking about their problems anonymously with another teen than they would in a more professional setting, face to face with a clinician. Teens at the hotline work to convince would-be suicide attempters that they have something to live for in their lives. They offer specific suggestions about where the teens can go to get help, and in critical situations, they try to find out where the teen is calling from so that they can send immediate help to intervene directly.

Hospitalization: when prevention efforts do not work

For some teens, prevention efforts have no effect, and many of those who fail in early suicide attempts will likely continue to try to take their lives until they succeed. These teens have moved beyond traditional prevention, and they should be viewed as patients in need of medical treatment. In these cases, mental health professionals sometimes choose hospitalization for teens.

The decision to hospitalize a teen is usually based on a number of factors. First, evaluators assess the likelihood of continued risk to the patient in the immediate future. Simon Davidson, professor and director of Child Psychiatric Research at Children's Hospital of Eastern Ontario, writes: "Information regarding the degree of risk includes: method used, degree of impairment of consciousness when rescued, extent of injury, time required in hospital to reverse the effects, and intensity of treatment required."[54] Clinicians may also choose hospitalization if a teen has a psychiatric disorder, such as depression, and also in cases where teens have no support systems outside of the hospital setting.

Doctors note that choosing to hospitalize teens after suicide attempts, and in some cases after threats of suicide, sends a message to the teen and his or her family that suicide is serious business. Even a brief stay in the hospital gives doctors a chance to assess the teen's current mental state; to treat and stabilize the teen's medical condition; to protect the teen for a short time by removing him or her from stressful social situations; to offer counseling for both the patient and his or her family; and to set up an outpatient treatment plan.

Talking it out: individual, group, and family therapy

Whether teens are hospitalized after their suicide attempts or not, they have a better chance of recovering from their suicidal tendencies if they enter into counseling or therapy. Teens who have not yet attempted suicide but are considering it may also benefit from it. There are a number of treatment plans available to teens, including individual therapy, group therapy with other teens, and family therapy.

Individual therapy is usually recommended for older teens whose problems are related less to home and family, than to peers or other interpersonal relationships. The length of individual treatment varies, depending on the teen's response to therapy. Treatment in therapy is directed towards what the teen needs most to return to a state of mental health. While one teen and her therapist might work on social skills and problem-solving training to conquer feelings of depression, for example, another teen might work to alleviate his feelings of loneliness or learn to manage his anger.

Cognitive-behavioral therapy is also a popular treatment option for teens. In this form of treatment teens are taught to monitor their own thoughts and behaviors in daily diaries. "From these observations might be constructed activity schedules, or systematic plans for decreasing negative and increasing positive thoughts and activities,"[55] note clinical psychology physicians Alan Berman and David Jobes. Teens can better focus on changing their negative thoughts about themselves or their self-destructive actions if they are more aware of the situations in which these thoughts or actions occur.

Teens who are placed in group therapy may work on many of the same behavior-changing skills as in individual therapy, but they do so in the presence of other suicidal peers. In groups, teens who have attempted or thought about committing suicide receive comfort and understanding from others like them. They may discuss their family or peer relationships, substance abuse problems, depression, and other factors that influence their mental health. Many teens in group therapy have refused family therapy because they know they will not find the support they need from home, or because they want to rebel. The group dynamic is helpful in that it affords teens an opportunity to make friends and increase their self-esteem.

Jose Jimenez is one teen who eventually benefited from both hospitalization after his last suicide attempt followed by group therapy sessions held at his high school. He was given time off from his English class to attend the sessions.

Teens who are depressed and suicidal can benefit from treatment programs such as hospitalization and therapy.

From eighth grade to eleventh, Jose had tried to kill himself on ten different occasions. His family did not know at
the time that he had been sexually abused by a relative for
eight years. In addition to the abuse and Jose's knowing
that his abuser had not been punished, his family and peers
criticized him for being gay. He tried to hang himself but
again failed to end his life. Sonia Nazario writes,

> During his month long hospitalization, Jose says, he was re-
> assured to see he wasn't the only suicidal teen. His roommate
> had poured gasoline over his head and set himself on fire. In-
> creasingly, Jose became angry at himself for allowing his mo-
> lester's actions to control his life. "I said never again will I be
> here. Not because of him."[56]

Later, in group therapy, Jose says he would pray with his
peers that their lives would get better. "We would cry in each
others' arms. We would try to encourage each other."[57]

While both individual and peer group therapy are helpful, they are usually not doctors' first choices for teens who
come from dysfunctional families, as many teens who
commit suicide do. If these teens are to succeed in their
treatment, their family dynamics will need to change. If
the family is willing to cooperate, family therapy is the
logical choice in these situations. It is also recommended
for younger teens and youth who attempt suicide.

The goal of family therapy is to change the way members
of dysfunctional families communicate and interact with
each other. Families are taught to improve their problem-
solving skills and to increase their support for the suicidal
adolescent by reinforcing appropriate, positive behaviors.

Through the development of suicide prevention and
treatment strategies, our society has done much to help
teens in crisis. Despite the many thousands of teens who
are helped each year through such programs, however,
there are still many who cannot be reached. Teens still take
their lives each year, and each year, more family and
friends are left grieving.

6

Postvention: Help for Survivors

TAKING INTO CONSIDERATION the fact that suicide prevention and treatment efforts are not always successful, mental health specialists have developed what is known as postvention, coping strategies for the families and friends of suicide victims. These suicide survivors, as they are called, find ways to pick up their lives and move on, even though they do not have all the answers about the deaths of their loved ones. Most survivors say that their lives are never the same; indeed, family units and friendships are often torn apart in the search for peace.

The painful aftermath of suicide

Perhaps if teens who have committed suicide imagined the pain and suffering their deaths would cause their loved ones, they would not have gone through with their acts. Unfortunately, the suicidal mind is not so rational. In the wake of suicide, the families and friends of teen victims are left feeling shocked and vulnerable.

Unlike grieving people who have lost loved ones due to natural causes, suicide survivors must face both the suddenness and violence of suicide. Even when families know their teens may be at risk for depression or even suicide, they are never prepared for teens to take their lives. The devastation they feel at the teens' premature deaths is not unlike those of parents who have lost their teens unexpectedly in car accidents or other tragedies. Similarly, family and friends must accept the violence of a suicide's death. Those who discover the victim are especially prone to reliving the scene, haunted by the images of death for years to come.

Survivors' shame

Some suicide survivors are unable to face the reality of suicide. Parents who have lost a child may cover up by telling friends the suicide was an accident, for example, or a homicide. These parents may stay in this state of denial for some time. Because of the stigma of suicide in our culture, a family may also suffer from extreme shame after a suicide.

The shame that accompanies suicide has a historical origin. In eighteenth-century Europe, for example, superstition dictated that the bodies of suicides be denied proper burial. Berman and Jobes explain, "To prevent the suicide's ghost from wandering, corpses have been decapitated, buried outside city limits or tribal territories, burned, beaten with chains, thrown to wild beasts, or buried at a crossroads with a stake through the heart."[58] Suicide survivors in those times might be forced to forfeit their goods and property to atone for the victim's sin, or to pay a fine to their in-laws for the shame the suicide had brought upon their family name.

Although our society is more accepting of suicide today, a stigma persists. Survivors may worry about what people in their community think about the situation. They may wonder whether rumors are spreading that all was not right at home; they may feel the family will no longer be respected in the community.

In addition to denial and fear about the social stigma of suicide, other survivors feel shame and guilt because they just could not do enough. One mother echoes the cries of hundreds of others when she speaks of her son's suicide. "I feel like I killed him," she says, "because I'm his mother and I should have saved him."[59] This kind of guilt is not uncommon among suicide survivors. And these feelings are magnified if the survivor had some kind of conflict with the victim before his or her death.

Survivors blame themselves for not being good enough parents, siblings, or friends. They ask themselves what

The parents and brother of a thirteen-year-old suicide victim are grief stricken after the teen's funeral. In addition to their sorrow, suicide survivors often harbor feelings of shame and guilt.

they might have done to push their loved one to suicide, and they replay the days and months leading up to the suicide, looking for the clues they regret not finding at the time. Finally, survivors may also feel guilt if the victim's method of suicide was readily available in the home—such as guns, medications, or other lethal means. Sometime survivors do not blame themselves, but others. They may blame God for not protecting loved ones, or blame therapists and other health care professionals who may have had a teen victim in their care. Survivors may blame aspects of society as well, like drugs, music, or the pressures of school.

Survivors in isolation

Suicide survivors feel a wide range of emotions that can ultimately affect their own mental health if they do not try to move beyond these feelings. Denial and guilt, for example, can quickly lead to depression. Survivors can also act out in ways that can be unhealthy for them as well. Often, survivors isolate themselves from others or refuse to pick back up with the pattern of their lives before the death. They may hide indoors, for example, or they may sell their homes and find new employment, in order to live among people who do not know their history. For some, these actions might lead to healing, but they might represent forms of denial as well. More importantly, suicide survivors are vulnerable, and may have thoughts of suicide themselves. They may not be able to foresee a future in which life is less painful.

Difficult survival

Ten years after Joe, her fourteen-year-old son, shot himself, Ann still grieves for him and recalls daily the argument she had with him about schoolwork on the day he died. Ann's own mental health was affected by the suicide, and her marriage suffered as well. Both of these effects are common in homes that have survived a suicide. For the first seven months after the suicide, Ann suffered from mental confusion. At traffic lights, she did not know whether to stop or go. She remembers wanting to kill herself to escape her pain, remembers also that she could not bear eating dinner with her family and seeing her son's empty place. It took her five years to stop laying out a table setting for him. Ann also wanted others to feel her pain. "I knew my husband was not responsible for Joe's death," she says, "but I did blame him." She told him he was a bad father because, "I wanted to see him in as much pain as I was in."[60] Although they still have their bad days, Ann's family was able to pull together and heal themselves through therapy, as many other suicide survivors have done.

Coping strategies

While the outlook for their lives may seem bleak, suicide survivors can cope with life after the death. These coping strategies can begin immediately with the funeral for the deceased. Traditional funerals allow for the display of emotions and offer the opportunity for friends and family to come together in support of each other. Death expert Elisabeth Kübler-Ross suggests that one way to help survivors cope is to create a memory table at the funeral, a place to display pictures and mementos of the teen to help loved ones remember his or her life. Some survivors might even take this opportunity to write letters to the deceased or to place their own mementos in the casket. Berman and Jobes suggest that not only can these actions positively affect the grief process, but that attempting to forgo mourning rituals can have negative results. "Attempts to play down the death limit the potential for wider social support—for the survivor, the suicide becomes a secret, and feelings of guilt, anger, and loss cannot be discussed with others who could help."[61]

Next, it is helpful if survivors do all they can to learn about suicide. Becoming familiar with suicide statistics and the causes of suicide often helps them put their lives in perspective as they grieve. Perhaps they will learn something that will offer some clues as to why the teen in their lives took his or her life. Survivors will also learn that the emotions they are feeling are common to other survivors. In the aftermath of suicide, they are not alone.

During the funeral for two teen suicide victims, friends and family of the deceased are able to express their anguish as well as receive support from fellow mourners.

As time passes, suicide survivors are reminded not to deny their own feelings. Extreme sadness does not go away, for instance, just because the funeral is over. Experts suggest grievers find a way to express these emotions by allowing themselves to cry when they need to. Surely survivors will feel renewed pain on the birthday of the teen they lost to suicide, and they may dread the anniversary of his or her death each year. Therapists advise that these dates should be celebrated, even through tears, rather than ignored. Ignoring them, they say, does not alleviate the pain. It is better to express the emotions these days elicit. Likewise, continuing feelings of anger and guilt should also be vented in a positive manner, rather than directed at others. Many survivors do this by volunteering their time for suicide prevention efforts.

Support for survivors

Just as suicidal teens often need professional support in their lives, so do the survivors of suicide. Some survivors feel that they may overburden their friends with their grieving and their need to repeatedly review the events of the suicide. In such cases, therapists may be able to offer the additional empathy survivors need. Professionals may also help survivors express their sadness or release their anger so that they may move forward in the stages of grieving.

Discussion groups made up of suicide survivors can also be as helpful as individual therapy, but some experts suggest that the group work should accompany therapy rather than replace it. Grief counselor Dr. Ellen Zinner notes that interestingly, these support groups are often more readily embraced by suicide survivors because the groups themselves are not clouded by the stigma that therapy sometimes carries.

Instead of feeling sick and in need of a therapist, survivors attend these support groups simply feeling in need. They also receive the added benefit of being able to help others. In these groups, Zinner writes,

> bereaved individuals can find real understanding and empathy, which normalizes feelings that may appear alien and

bizarre. No matter what feeling or behavior is expressed, there are always people nodding their head in affirmation, assuring that they, too, know what this experience is like.[62]

Political action and consumer advocacy also often grow out of suicide survivors' groups. Groups might involve themselves in gun control efforts, for example, or take on the issue of violence in the media.

Postvention in the schools

When a teen takes his or her life, the effects can be far reaching. It is not only the immediate family and friends of the teen whose lives are changed by suicide, but also his or her classmates. These teens may experience feelings of anxiety, depression, and guilt even if they were not especially close to the teen who committed suicide. Therefore, they are also in need of postvention efforts—just as prevention works to help avoid suicide, postvention occurs after the suicide.

For postvention efforts to work best on school grounds, school principals should immediately recognize that a problem exists. Many mental health experts agree that a school should deal with the subject of a teen's suicide both openly and honestly. Even if the normal routine of the school is disrupted for a few days, researchers find that the time spent on these postvention efforts is well worth the disruption. School personnel should be trained for such crises in advance, and encouraged to create a forum in which teens can discuss their own feelings about suicide.

Therapists who support postvention attempts at school say that teachers and school administrators should strive to prevent other teens from identifying with the suicide victim. Although teens may want to discuss what a wonderful person the teen was and how much the teen had going for him or her, experts say, it is best to recall the negative aspects of the teen's life as well. The negative social, emotional, psychological, or family problems leading up to the suicide should be expressed so that other teens do not feel that the suicide was the choice of a healthy, stable mind. Mental health professionals note that school officials should review all of the risk factors of suicide with teens, and work to prevent students from romanticizing or glorifying the recent event.

Special crisis teams may also be set up on campus to help faculty and other staff members to counsel teens in need. Teens are best served in situations where those who run the school are well prepared and are themselves able to cope in the aftermath of suicide. Suicidologists warn that crisis team members should be alert to other students who may be at risk and influenced by the recent suicide. Siblings, other relatives, and close friends of the victim may be at risk for suicide themselves and will likely need the most comfort.

Even students who did not know the deceased can be at risk if they have lost someone to suicide in the past or if they have considered or attempted suicide themselves. Other teens at risk might be those who helped in any way with the suicide plans of the victim, perhaps by helping to write the suicide note or helping give things away. Students who knew of plans for the suicide in advance might also feel guilty and suicidal for not telling others. Other guilty feelings may arise from teens who felt it was their responsibility to keep their friend alive; still others may feel responsible for the death because of the way they treated the teen or for recent arguments they may have had with him or her.

The will to survive

Postvention efforts can help give suicide survivors the strength and will to live on without their loved ones. This change does not come easily, but the American Association of Suicidology reminds survivors that they can cope with their loss. Suicidologists advise survivors to take their lives one moment or one day at a time for as long as they need to in order to regain a sense of stability. It takes time to heal. Survivors should not feel shame in not feeling able to make major decisions about their lives while they are grieving, and they should not feel alarmed if they experience setbacks during the grieving process. Finally, mental

In the aftermath of a suicide, survivors must find ways to cope with the loss of their loved one and regain their will to survive.

health experts remind survivors that letting go of their loved one does not mean forgetting that person. And once they can achieve this step, survivors will eventually find that they move beyond simply surviving to a renewed interest and joy in their lives.

Suicide survivors are not the only ones who can benefit from harnessing their will to survive. At-risk teens can do the same. Teens who are depressed or abused, those misusing drugs or alcohol, those caught in confusing dysfunctional family settings or lost in the swirl of their own interpersonal, financial, or legal problems, can all find help for the problems that trouble them.

Today society can work to help these teens not only by continuing to educate them and their loved ones in suicide prevention programs, but also by working to alleviate the core causes of teen suicide by taking each of these issues in hand and preventing them from overpowering teens. Through these efforts, at-risk teens can regain their self-esteem. They might awaken to a new hope in their lives, eager to meet each new day.

Notes

Chapter 1: Teen Suicide Rates Are on the Rise

1. Sonia Nazario, "Children Who Kill Themselves," *Los Angeles Times*, March 9, 1997, p. A1+.

2. Nazario, "Children Who Kill Themselves."

3. John M. Davis and Jonathan Sandoval, *Suicidal Youth*. San Francisco: Jossey-Bass, 1991, p. 115.

4. Quoted in Fern Shen, "Suicides Rise for Young Black Males; Various Reasons Offered for Increasing Rates," *Washington Post*, July 21, 1996, p. B1+.

5. Shen, "Suicides Rise for Young Black Males."

6. Quoted in *Jet*, "Why Suicide Is Increasing Among Young Black Men," August 12, 1996, p. 12+.

7. Quoted in Shen, "Suicides Rise for Young Black Males."

8. Quoted in *Jet*, "Why Suicide Is Increasing Among Young Black Men."

9. Quoted in *Jet*, "Why Suicide Is Increasing Among Young Black Men."

10. Quoted in Tamara L. Roleff, ed., *Suicide: Opposing Viewpoints*. San Diego: Greenhaven Press, 1998, p. 68.

11. Delia M. Rios, "A Bogus Statistic That Won't Go Away," *American Journalism Review*, July/August 1997, p. 12+.

12. Quoted in Rios, "A Bogus Statistic That Won't Go Away."

13. Quoted in Rachel A. Vannatta, "Adolescent Gender Differences in Suicide-Related Behaviors," *Journal of Youth and Adolescence*, October 1997, p. 559+.

14. Quoted in Vannatta, "Adolescent Gender Differences in Suicide-Related Behaviors."

Chapter 2: Inner Conflicts

15. Robert M. Cavanaugh Jr., William L. Licamele, Christopher R. Ovide, and Cynthia Starr, "What's Normal and What's Not: Teen Mental Health," *Patient Care*, June 15, 1997, p. 82+.

16. *USA Today Magazine*, "Adults Should Heed Teens' Warning Signs," December 1997, p. 4.

17. Quoted in Janice Arenofsky, "Teen Suicide: When the Blues Get Out of Control," *Current Health 2*, December 1997, p. 16+.

18. Quoted in Arenofsky, "Teen Suicide: When the Blues Get Out of Control."

19. Quoted in Nazario, "Children Who Kill Themselves."

20. Quoted in Nazario, "Children Who Kill Themselves."

21. Herbert Hendin, *Suicide in America.* New York: Norton, 1995, p. 74.

22. Hendin, *Suicide in America*, p. 63.

23. Quoted in Hendin, *Suicide in America*, p. 72.

24. Quoted in Robert Emmet Long, ed., *The Reference Shelf: Suicide*. New York: H. W. Wilson, 1995, p. 11.

25. Quoted in Long, *The Reference Shelf: Suicide*, p. 11.

26. Quoted in George MacLean, ed., *Suicide in Children and Adolescents*. Toronto: Hogrefe & Huber, 1990, p. 81.

27. Quoted in Alan L. Berman and David A. Jobes, *Adolescent Suicide Assessment and Intervention*. Washington, DC: American Psychological Association, 1991, p. 95.

28. Quoted in *New York Times*, "Burdened by Speeding Fine, a Boy Takes His Life," April 13, 1995, p. A22.

Chapter 3: Outside Influences

29. Quoted in Loren Coleman, *Suicide Clusters*. Boston: Faber and Faber, 1987, p. 99.

30. Quoted in Coleman, *Suicide Clusters*, p. 100.

31. Quoted in Coleman, *Suicide Clusters*, p. 106.

32. Steven Stack, Jim Gundlach, and Jimmie L. Reeves, "The Heavy Metal Subculture and Suicide," *Suicide and Life Threatening Behavior*, Spring 1994, p. 18.

33. Stack, Gundlach, and Reeves, "The Heavy Metal Subculture and Suicide," p. 16.

34. Quoted in Stack, Gundlach, and Reeves, "The Heavy Metal Subculture and Suicide," p. 22.

35. Philip Patros and Tonia Shamoo, *Depression and Suicide in Children and Adolescents*. Boston: Allyn and Bacon, 1989, p. 59.

Chapter 4: Suicide Phenomena

36. Ron Arias, "The Lost Daughters: After a Teen Suicide Pact, Two Families Cope with Their Grief—and Unanswered Questions," *People Weekly*, September 18, 1995, p. 60+.

37. Quoted in Arias, "The Lost Daughters."

38. Quoted in Arias, "The Lost Daughters."

39. Quoted in Coleman, *Suicide Clusters*, p. 89.

40. Quoted in Coleman, *Suicide Clusters*, p. 90.

41. Quoted in Arias, "The Lost Daughters."

42. Quoted in Pam Belluck, "In Little City Safe from Violence, Rash of Suicides Leaves Scars," *New York Times*, April 5, 1998, p. A1.

43. Margaret Nelson, "A Reason to Live," *Teen People*, November 1998, p. 71.

44. Quoted in Nelson, "A Reason to Live," p. 71.

45. Centers for Disease Control and Prevention, "Suicide Contagion and the Reporting of Suicide: Recommendations from a National Workshop," *Morbidity and Mortality Weekly Report*, April 22, 1994, p. 16.

46. Centers for Disease Control and Prevention, "Suicide Contagion and the Reporting of Suicide," p. 16.

47. Centers for Disease Control and Prevention, "Suicide Contagion and the Reporting of Suicide," p. 17.

Chapter 5: Prevention Programs and Treatment

48. Lloyd B. Potter, Mark L. Rosenberg, and W. Rodney Hammond, "Suicide in Youth: A Public Framework," *Journal of the American Academy of Child and Adolescent Psychiatry*, May 1998, p. 486.

49. Quoted in Arenofsky, "Teen Suicide: When the Blues Get Out of Control."

50. Quoted in *Brown University Child and Adolescent Behavior Letter*, "Grief Turns Into Action in Washington State," June 1997, p. 3+.

51. Quoted in Sonia Nazario, "Schools Struggle to Teach Lessons in Life and Death," *Los Angeles Times*, March 10, 1997, p. A1+.

52. Quoted in Nazario, "Schools Struggle to Teach Lessons in Life and Death."

53. Quoted in Nazario, "Schools Struggle to Teach Lessons in Life and Death."

54. Quoted in MacLean, *Suicide in Children and Adolescents*, p. 105.

55. Berman and Jobes, *Adolescent Suicide Assessment and Intervention*, p. 203.

56. Nazario, "Children Who Kill Themselves."

57. Quoted in Nazario, "Children Who Kill Themselves."

Chapter 6: Postvention: Help for Survivors

58. Berman and Jobes, *Adolescent Suicide Assessment and Intervention*, p. 245.

59. Quoted in Nazario, "Children Who Kill Themselves."

60. Quoted in Nazario, "Children Who Kill Themselves."

61. Berman and Jobes, *Adolescent Suicide Assessment and Intervention*, p. 250.

62. Quoted in Peter Cimbolic and David A. Jobes, eds., *Youth Suicide: Issues, Assessment, and Intervention*. Springfield, IL: Charles C. Thomas, 1990, p. 82.

Organizations to Contact

The following resources offer information on suicide and suicide prevention. Those who need immediate assistance, for themselves or someone they know, can seek the help of any healthcare professional or can obtain a number for a 24-hour suicide prevention hotline by consulting the Community Services section of the local phone directory.

The American Association of Suicidology
4201 Connecticut Ave. NW, Suite 310
Washington, DC 20008
(202) 237-2250
Internet: www.suicidology.org/

The American Association of Suicidology is a nonprofit organization dedicated to the understanding and prevention of suicide. This association offers resources for anyone concerned about suicide, including suicide researchers, therapists, prevention specialists, survivors of suicide, and people in crisis.

American Foundation for Suicide Prevention
120 Wall St. 22nd Floor
New York, NY 10005
(212) 410-1111

The foundation supports research on depression and suicide, provides public education, and offers support for suicide survivors.

National Center for Injury Prevention and Control
Division of Violence Prevention
Centers for Disease Control and Prevention

Mailstop K60
4770 Buford Hwy.
Atlanta, GA 30341-3724
(770) 488-4362

The center provides a variety of suicide prevention resource materials free of charge.

National Committee on Youth Suicide Prevention

825 Washington St.
Norwood, MA 02062
(617) 769-5686

The committee provides a range of materials in an effort to prevent suicide among youths and teens.

Samaritans

500 Commonwealth Ave.
Boston, MA 02215
(617) 247-0220

Samaritans is the largest suicide prevention organization in the world. Volunteers provide counseling and crisis assistance to suicidal people of all ages.

SA\VE—Suicide Awareness\Voices of Education

P.O. Box 24507
Minneapolis, MN 55424-0507
(612) 946-7998

This suicide prevention organization publishes pamphlets, books, and newsletters on suicide prevention and survival. It especially works to comfort and educate those who have lost loved ones to suicide.

Youth Suicide Nation Center

445 Virginia Ave.
San Mateo, CA 94402
(415) 655-1974

This center coordinates and supports youth suicide prevention programs. It develops and distributes educational materials on the subject.

Websites

These sites are helpful for people interested in learning more about suicide, suicide prevention, and other teen issues. Some sites offer suicide crisis information, but they should not be used in place of seeking professional services in your area.

The Jason Foundation

www.geocities.com/~jasnfoundation/mission.html

The Jason Foundation helps educate parents, teachers, other youth workers, and teens about teen suicide. Their preventative program, "A Promise for Tomorrow," is designed to help teens deal with the pressures of growing up and offers a choice other than suicide as an answer to problems.

Suicide Information and Education Center

www.siec.ca/

Established in 1982, the SIEC boasts the world's largest English language collection on suicidal behaviors, containing more than twenty-four thousand print and audiovisual materials on all aspects of suicidal behavior.

Teen Advice Online

www.teenadviceonline.org

Teen Advice Online provides support for teens through a network of peers worldwide. The site is run not by health care professionals but by teens thirteen and older who offer advice for common teen problems.

The Yellow Ribbon Organization

www.yellowribbon.org

This site contains information on teen suicide prevention especially and discusses the Yellow Ribbon card program begun in Colorado. The cards can be modified and printed from this source.

Suggestions for Further Reading

Warren Colman, *Understanding and Preventing Teen Suicide*. Chicago: Childrens Press, 1990. Colman examines causes of teen depression and other aspects of teen suicide in this succinct overview; includes color photographs.

Stephen A. Flanders, *Suicide*. New York: Facts On File, 1991. A historical look at suicide from biblical times to the twentieth century. The author includes statistics on suicide in the United States and examines causes, treatment, and prevention of suicide.

Dorothy B. Francis, *Suicide: A Preventable Tragedy*. New York: Dutton, 1989. Information and guidance on the warning signs of teen suicide, support groups, and local and national organizations for the prevention of suicide.

Bernard Frankel and Rachel Kranz, *Straight Talk About Teenage Suicide*. New York: Facts On File, 1994. Useful information for teens on stress, depression, suicide, and suicide prevention.

Sandra Gardner, *Teenage Suicide*. Englewood Cliffs, NJ: Julian Messner, 1990. Written in consultation with Dr. Gary Rosenberg, this book works to dispel the myths that surround teen suicide. Risk factors and prevention are discussed.

Patricia Hermes, *A Time to Listen: Preventing Youth Suicide*. San Diego: Harcourt, 1987. Using interviews with teens who have attempted suicide, depressed teens, suicide survivors, and therapists, Hermes examines teen suicide issues.

Cynthia Copeland Lewis, *Teen Suicide: Too Young to Die.* Hillside, NJ: Enslow, 1994. Lewis defines and examines teen suicide, suicide prevention, and suicide survivors in this easy-to-read text.

Works Consulted

Books

Alan L. Berman and David A. Jobes, *Adolescent Suicide Assessment and Intervention.* Washington, DC: American Psychological Association, 1991. A scholarly text, this book contains chapters on epidemiology, suicide theories, early detection, treatment, and prevention and postvention.

Peter Cimbolic and David A. Jobes, eds., *Youth Suicide: Issues, Assessment, and Intervention.* Springfield, IL: Charles C. Thomas, 1990.

Loren Coleman, *Suicide Clusters.* Boston: Faber and Faber, 1987. This book thoroughly explores the phenomenon of suicide clusters from ancient Greece through the 1980s. One chapter focuses specifically on teens.

John M. Davis and Jonathan Sandoval, *Suicidal Youth.* San Francisco: Jossey-Bass, 1991. This text about suicidal teens is meant to enable schools to set up programs for suicide screening, evaluation, prevention, and postvention.

Herbert Hendin, *Suicide in America.* New York: Norton, 1995. Written by a member of the American Suicide Foundation, this text offers a thorough discussion of suicide in America. It includes one chapter on suicide among the young.

David Lester, *Why People Kill Themselves: A 1990s Summary of Research Findings on Suicidal Behavior.* Springfield, IL: Charles C. Thomas, 1992. At the forefront of research in suicidology, David Lester reviews theories and research published on suicide in the 1980s in this extensive volume.

Robert Emmet Long, ed., *The Reference Shelf: Suicide.* New York: H. W. Wilson, 1995. Contains fifteen articles on suicide collected from a variety of U.S. sources. In addition to articles about teens, the book contains views on assisted suicide.

George MacLean, ed., *Suicide in Children and Adolescents.* Toronto: Hogrefe & Huber, 1990. A collection of articles written by medical doctors on topics including epidemiology, clinical perspectives, depressive disorders, risk factors, and management of suicidal adolescents.

Philip Patros and Tonia Shamoo, *Depression and Suicide in Children and Adolescents.* Boston: Allyn and Bacon, 1989. An especially thorough discussion on teens and depression. Other topics handled in depth include suicide prevention and postvention issues.

Tamara L. Roleff, ed., *Suicide: Opposing Viewpoints.* San Diego: Greenhaven Press, 1998. This collection of issues on suicide includes a section on teen suicide. Topics include: the role of guns in teen suicides, homosexual teens at risk, and depression.

James K. Zimmerman and Gregory M. Asnis, eds., *Treatment Approaches with Suicidal Adolescents.* New York: Wiley-Interscience, 1995. The editors have collected a variety of scholarly articles written by and for therapists treating suicidal adolescents.

Periodicals and Internet Sources

Advocate, "Youth at Risk," October 14, 1997.

Janice Arenofsky, "Teen Suicide: When the Blues Get Out of Control," *Current Health 2*, December 1997.

Ron Arias, "The Lost Daughters: After a Teen Suicide Pact, Two Families Cope with Their Grief—and Unanswered Questions," *People Weekly*, September 18, 1995.

Pam Belluck, "In Little City Safe from Violence, Rash of Suicides Leaves Scars," *New York Times*, April 5, 1998.

Iris M. Bolton, "Beyond Surviving: Suggestions for Survivors," American Association of Suicidology, 1998. www.cyberpsych.org/

Brown University Child and Adolescent Behavior Letter, "Grief Turns Into Action in Washington State," June 1997.

Robert M. Cavanaugh Jr., William L. Licamele, Christopher R. Ovide, and Cynthia Starr, "What's Normal and What's Not: Teen Mental Health," *Patient Care*, June 15, 1997.

Centers for Disease Control and Prevention, "Suicide Contagion and the Reporting of Suicide: Recommendations from a National Workshop," *Morbidity and Mortality Weekly Report*, April 22, 1994.

Jet, "Why Suicide Is Increasing Among Young Black Men," August 12, 1996.

Los Angeles Times, "The Victims," March 9, 1997.

Alexandra Marks, "Rise in Teen Suicides Spurs New Solutions," *Christian Science Monitor*, March 5, 1997.

Sonia Nazario, "Children Who Kill Themselves," *Los Angeles Times*, March 9, 1997.

Sonia Nazario, "Schools Struggle to Teach Lessons in Life and Death," *Los Angeles Times*, March 10, 1997.

Margaret Nelson, "A Reason to Live," *Teen People*, November 1998.

New York Times, "Burdened by Speeding Fine, a Boy Takes His Life," April 13, 1995.

Lloyd B. Potter, Mark L. Rosenberg, and W. Rodney Hammond, "Suicide in Youth: A Public Framework," *Journal of the American Academy of Child and Adolescent Psychiatry*, May 1998.

Delia M. Rios, "A Bogus Statistic That Won't Go Away," *American Journalism Review*, July/August 1997.

Fern Shen, "Suicides Rise for Young Black Males; Various Reasons Offered for Increasing Rates," *Washington Post*, July 21, 1996.

Steven Stack, Jim Gundlach, and Jimmie L. Reeves, "The Heavy Metal Subculture and Suicide," *Suicide and Life Threatening Behavior*, Spring 1994.

USA Today Magazine, "Adults Should Heed Teens' Warning Signs," December 1997.

Rachel A. Vannatta, "Adolescent Gender Differences in Suicide-Related Behaviors," *Journal of Youth and Adolescence*, October 1997.

Index

Picture Credits

Cover photo: © The Stock Market/Robert Essel
© 1992 Consolidated News Pictures/Ron Sachs/Archive
  Photos, 63
AP/Wideworld Photos, 46, 59, 71, 73, 77
Archive Photos, 36
Corbis/AFP, 53, 54
Corbis/Lynn Goldsmith, 39
Digital Stock, 18, 32
Carl Franzén, 12, 17
PhotoDisc, 7, 11, 24, 28, 29, 31, 41, 57, 62
© Rick Reinhard/Impact Visuals 1993, 44
Theodore E. Roseen, 67
UPI/Bettman, 49

About the Author

Hayley R. Mitchell holds a master of fine arts degree in po-
etry from the University of Washington and master's degree
in literature from California State University, Long Beach.
She teaches college-level creative writing and composition in
Southern California and edits the small press literary magazine, *Sheila-Na-Gig*. Her other titles for Lucent Books include *Teen Alcoholism* and *The Wolf*, and she has edited two
literary companions for Greenhaven Press: *Readings on:
Wuthering Heights* and *Readings on: A Doll's House*.